Pistol WHIPPED

A Sexy Millionaire Romance

STEFANIE GRAHAM

PISTOL WHIPPED
Copyright © 2021 by Stefanie Graham

ISBN: 978-0-9858189-7-5 (eBook)
        978-0-9858189-6-8 (Paperback)

Library or Congress Number: 2020922994

Cover Image by Shutterstock
Edited by Daisycakes Creative Services

Printed in the United States of America
First Printing Edition January 2021

About The Author

STEFANIE GRAHAM made her first attempt at writing romances at sixteen. She spent her proceeding years dreaming of ways to create the essence of passion and desire between pages filled with sultry and exciting text. She is a voracious reader; a fan of the written word in all forms and is happiest when curled up in a corner with a good book. Her goal is to create quality multi-genre titles that will capture the imagination of her readers. Stefanie enjoys traveling above all else and plans to visit every corner of the earth. Until then, she calls the East Coast her home.

Stefanie Graham loves to hear from her readers, if you want to chat, she's easy to find!

Twitter @ AuthorStefanieG
Instagram @ AuthorStefanieG
Facebook @ AuthorStefanieGraham
Website: www.StefanieGraham.com

ALSO BY STEFANIE GRAHAM
TROPICAL STORM

Acknowledgment

This book is dedicated to my friend, indie author Yvonne Harriott. Cancer stole you away, but it's your voice in my head that motivates me. I still delight in the fact that when you first read the draft for this book, you found the premise a tad bit naughty and risqué. It makes me happy to picture you in heaven clutching celestial pearls while secretly reading my final copy. It is my great honor to have known you.

Whipped ~ Slang for when a dominant woman has a man do anything she desires.
(Source - Urban Dictionary)

Chapter One

The new owner of Avion Industries distracted himself from the moving boxes piled high all around him by taking in the panoramic view of the downtown Toronto skyline. From where he stood, all Austin DeAngelis could see were endless rows of glass and steel office buildings fighting a silent battle against the glaring heat of the late summer sun. To him, the buildings were like living entities stretching high beyond the clouds, as if elevation alone gave them dominion over the lush green trees and the manicured perfection of the landscapes far below.

Turning away from the view, Austin studied his new employees through the floor-to-ceiling clear glass windows. A woman, one of his few female employees if the staff directory was correct, caught and riveted his attention. An unfamiliar awareness simmering through him made him question why. He moved to get a better look at her, but a

1

man appeared on her left, partially blocking his view. A conversation ensued, but even from where he stood, it was obvious the woman wasn't listening.

Briefly studying the man, Austin observed that the New Age nerd didn't wear pencil protectors like in reruns of old eighties movies. They'd evolved. These days, they made apps and designed video games; they were innovators. It was true that the waists of their jeans were still a tad too close to their belly buttons to be considered fashionable, but today's *Smart Guy* had come a long way. Their taste in women was a case in point. Almost compulsively, his gaze was drawn back to the woman. She held both his and her admirer's attention. He guessed the man was one of his programmers, although he'd never personally met any of the staff. What he knew of his employee already was that he had a refined and distinguished palate. If he was reppin' for the geek squad, then it was obvious that the airhead prom queen or the dim but leggy model of old just wouldn't do. When it came to seeking validation, today's *technical intellectual* wanted a woman with both beauty and brains. If the fiercely intense way the man looked at the woman was any indication, she had both assets in spades.

"Hi there."

Kylie Derringer-DeValle nodded in greeting but didn't look up from her computer. *Why did the Tech team insist on making last-minute changes?* The new specs that had landed in her inbox that morning meant that instead of being ahead of schedule, she was now behind with a looming deadline.

A shadow darkened her screen and she frowned, puzzled. Lord, if the monitor died now... Before she could reach out to adjust it, someone cleared their throat. Startled, she looked up and found the senior programmer, Jim, propped against her desk, hip jutted out at what seemed to be an awkward angle.

She removed her glasses and tucked them into her hair. Seconds ticked by. When Jim remained silent, she decided to help him out, offering a brief smile. "Yes?"

His gaze widened and his lips moved silently but nothing came out. Her irritation flared.

Why do I even bother? After a year of contracting at Avion, she had hoped her coworkers would warm up to her and stop treating her like an alien. Obviously, that was too much to ask.

"Do you need something, Jim?" she said hearing the resignation in her tone. She replaced her glasses and turned back to the computer. If he wasn't going to be polite, neither would she.

"Well, Ms. DeValle, we were wondering when you'd have the latest version of the software manual ready?"

That does it. Slowly, she spun her chair around and pinned the older man with her gaze. She'd been told the glasses magnified the coldness of her gray eyes and she often used that to her advantage in negotiations.

"How long have I worked here?"

Sweat beaded his upper lip and his eyes darted behind her as if seeking rescue. He shifted and gulped. "Uh, three hundred and sixty-two days, six hours, and a few minutes. I'm guessing," he added hurriedly when her eyebrows rose.

Stalker much? Kylie resisted the urge to edge her chair away from him.

"And how many times have I told you not to use my second name? Call me Ms. Derringer, or Kylie if you want."

"Right. Sure thing, uh, Ms. Derringer." He was backing away, not really looking. She sighed.

"Jim." He flinched to a stop, nearly colliding with a rolling cart filled with binders and copy paper. "You wanted to know about the manual?" When he didn't reply, just stared, she resisted the urge to sigh again. "You'll have it on Monday. The team made some last-minute changes. That's the only reason it's not completed already."

"Of course. Thank you, uh, ma'am."

"Call me Kylie," she said to his retreating back. Turning back to her computer, she murmured, "After all, you are my boss."

She began typing but her fingers slowed when the loud whispers from Jim and his programmers drifted to her from where they'd gathered across the room.

"What did she say?" one quavering voice asked.

"She said she would have it done by Monday," Jim answered with an authority he'd failed to show even seconds ago. "But the next time we draw straws to decide who has to talk to her, I'm drawing first."

She heard murmurs of agreement and commiseration in the answering voices and buried the twinge of hurt she felt inside.

"Who is that?" Austin DeAngelis asked as his second-in-command entered his office, interrupting his voyeuristic moment.

Brixton Castlemaine glanced over his shoulder. "That's Kylie Derringer-DeValle, your senior technical writer," he answered his friend and boss cheerfully. "She's the best documentation specialist this company has ever had, but she is a little hard to get along with."

"So I see." Austin's eyes swept over what he imagined were lush curves hidden beneath an oversized cardigan.

Brixton waved his hand in front of his friend's face to divert his attention. "I know what you're thinking. Forget it," he advised. "Kylie is more than a handful. She has a tongue like a serpent, a mind like a steel trap, and an attitude that will stop any man cold. A pretty package on the outside but she has a disposition that will tear a man's balls off."

Austin threw his head back and exploded into laughter. "You've been here less than two months to oversee this takeover and you know her that well already?" He couldn't help but be intrigued.

His friend's grimace spoke of thwarted romantic attempts and Austin laughed even harder. Shaking his head, he said, "Thanks for the warning. No need though. Although I just acquired this company, I'm still the new kid on the block. Somehow, I think dating my female employees is a bad way to start. Besides, you know I like my women tame, quiet, and biddable. From the looks of that troublemaker, she doesn't have my required temperament."

Austin's eyes slid compulsively back to the woman who sat, seemingly comfortable and at home, stuffed in a tiny cubicle away from everyone else. "She *is* beautiful though," he said absently. His eyes caressed her from the top of her shining hair to the tips of her toe-stomping combat boots.

Brixton grunted at this assessment. "Yeah well, an AK-47 is beautiful too, but that doesn't mean I want to put my face in front of one."

"Good point," Austin admitted. "I wonder, though, how one very tiny woman can put so much fear into the hearts of a company full of men."

"You don't have to wonder. Let me introduce you. I'm curious to see if like the other women in your life she'll take one look at you and fall on her back with her legs spread." Brixton's tone was clearly skeptical.

"Goes to show how much you know," Austin chuckled. "Instantaneous spread-eagle is both vulgar and atypical. The women of my acquaintance are ladies. If legs are spreading, it's done with style."

Brixton rolled his eyes and made a sweeping gesture toward the door with his hand.

"Fine. Whatever," Austin agreed. He accepted the silent challenge. His expression suggested boredom, but he felt goosebumps on his skin.

She was even more beautiful up close. Everything about her was pint-sized. She had a small nose, tiny hands, a petite figure, and little feet. What was big about her were the things that could make any healthy man salivate. She had big metallic-grey eyes — the color of steel and storms, a luxurious mass of honey and copper-colored hair, and breasts that would be average on most females but were immense on a frame no bigger than a child's. Separate, her attributes were disproportionate and uninteresting, but together they were the stuff of a *Playboy* magazine centerfold. He could tell she would be easy to pick up and position and ...

Austin snapped his mind back to the introduction at hand. He'd always had a weakness for beautiful women but one this tiny was out of the question. He stayed away from petite ladies. In his experience, they generally couldn't handle him sexually. He was a big man, not just in height, so he preferred bed partners who'd been around, knew the ropes, and liked a challenge. Everyday women had a hard time; a woman the size of this one, would make what he wanted to do to her impossible. The care it would take—the patience. He'd have to go slow, prepare her properly and even then, a pleasurable outcome wasn't guaranteed. Austin sighed and let the thought slip away. It was pointless fantasizing. It would never work. He knew it, but still, he couldn't help himself. His gaze drifted back to his new employee and his eyebrows shot up with surprise when her eyes met his.

She was scowling. Not scowling exactly but her expression was partly a grimace and partly a baring of teeth.

Eyes narrowed and mouth pursed, she slowly, deliberately closed the edges of her sweater with a jerk, blocking out his gaze. Despite the dubious start to their acquaintance, Austin still awaited the inevitable blinking look he usually received when the opposite sex got the first good look at his face. Her expression didn't change. It was just short of openly hostile. Austin was momentarily disconcerted. Not every woman found him attractive but ninety-five percent of them did. He took it for granted. There were women who weren't affected by his looks, but those individuals were rare. For instance, ninety-year-old grandmothers sometimes didn't bat an eye; they were too old to care. Sometimes, ladies who loved the ladies didn't look at him twice. Even then he'd been able to convince some of these women that they could find pleasure by switching back to the other side, if even briefly. He had that effect on women, but apparently not on this one.

A smile of amusement instantly lit his face. She hated him...on sight. How interesting.

"Nice to meet you, Ms. DeValle," he said, recovering gracefully. "I hear you are the best writer that Avion Industries has ever had. I'm pleased to have such a talented staff member on my team." Despite himself, Austin gave her the ten-volt lady-killer smile.

It was unappreciated.

"My name is Ms. Derringer. I don't use the second surname anymore," she explained firmly, looking him directly in the eyes. Their gazes battled for a second more before Kylie turned her chair back towards her computer screen. Apparently, the conversation was at a close.

"Derringer. Isn't that the name of a nineteenth-century gun?" He was doing his best to draw her attention back to him. "If I'm not mistaken, it was the smallest useable handgun of its time which is what made it popular with the ladies of that era. Easy to conceal and beautifully crafted; a diminutive and dainty piece of steel innocuous enough to fool the unsuspecting into thinking it was something other than a lethal weapon."

Her chair slowly spun back around. The eyes that stared at him showed surprise — the barest hint of interest.

Austin quietly patted himself on the back for having a head for inconsequential details.

"A Derringer is a gun. Not many people know the history behind the handgun. How is it that you do?" Her voice was raspy and slightly masculine which was so completely at odds with the rest of her that the effect was somehow erotic. Her throaty rumble had the same effect on him as a soft hand on bare skin.

Austin heard Brixton draw in an astonished breath. At that moment, he was aware that he had accomplished the impossible — gaining Kylie Derringer's full attention.

Austin unconsciously turned up the voltage of his smile. "I dunno." He shrugged. "I think I read it somewhere. I didn't know at the time the information would come in handy." Despite himself, his eyes slid over her appreciatively.

The interest in her eyes died by degrees. "Well," she said contemplating him through narrowed eyelids, "it's good to know that the new owner can read." With that, she swiveled her chair back to her screen again and silently dismissed them.

"Jesus Christ! Where did you get that ballbuster from?" Austin exclaimed when they were safely back in his office.

"I told you," Brixton smirked, rubbing it in.

"Yeah, you told me. I thought you were exaggerating." Austin laughed.

"No need to exaggerate in Kylie's case. She's every man's worst nightmare: beautiful, talented, intelligent, and aggressively off-limits. If we leave her alone to do her job and stay out of her way, it works best for all of us. Kylie doesn't like men."

Austin's brows shot up. "Lesbian?" he inquired.

11

Brixton laughed. "No, I don't think so. According to office gossip, there was a boyfriend of some kind a while ago. That doesn't seem to change the fact that she's not that fond of those of us who pee standing up though."

"Interesting," Austin mused. His eyes wandered back to the spot where the only female employee on his tech team sat huddled in a corner yards away from any of her coworkers.

What a waste. He sighed again and then dismissed Kylie Derringer from his thoughts.

Chapter Two

Kylie's combat boots made thumping noises on the pavement and her black leggings, affixed with multiple, mini, metal chains rattled as she walked towards the intersection of Jane and Finch Street in the Northwest end of Toronto. She'd left her car down the block as parking was a nightmare anywhere near her mom's building. The closer she got to the old neighborhood, the more conscious she became of her surroundings. Her eyes were more alert, she kept her hands at her sides, her posture got straighter, and her expression became fixed and remote. Although it mostly got a bad rap, that didn't change the fact that her former address was best known for its yellow police tape and news cameras. Keeping her thoughts on the visit ahead, she passed the local shops, nail salons, fast food joints that lined both sides of the streets and approached the apartment building where she'd spent her formative years. Without knowing it, her straight shoulders drooped, her steps slowed, and a frown marred the smoothness of her brow.

If the pissy hallways, the elevator buttons that always had something unimaginable smeared across them, and the unsavory characters loitering around weren't enough to depress her spirits, her mother hanging half-drunk off the sofa when she walked through the door did the trick.

"Hello, Mom," Kylie said softly startling awake the woman who'd been sprawled in front of the television. Her mother pushed her once-lush locks away from her face and struggled to her feet. Kylie knew better than to help her. Digging chipped toenails vandalized by smeared blood-red nail polish into her slippers, she walked over to her daughter. Kylie stood in silence as her mother tied her tattered bathrobe around her body before shooting a guilty look across the room. Discarded wine bottles lay scattered over the rug.

"Kylie, darling, what are you doing here? Is it Thursday already?" Lana Derringer rubbed her bloodshot eyes with the back of her hand. "Don't stand at the door, honey. Come over here and give your mother a hug." She opened her arms and smiled broadly. For a split second, the smile dimmed the reality of her appearance, brightening her blue eyes and lighting up her face. In that moment, Kylie had a direct glimpse at the face she remembered from her childhood. Plastering a smile on her face, Kylie stepped into her mother's embrace. The internal countdown started almost immediately. She waited until she reached ten before she released herself from the smell of cheap perfume and stale alcohol.

Her mother released her and stepped back to give her daughter the once-over. "Kylie, why won't you wear a dress? You'd look so pretty in a dress," she complained.

Kylie shifted restlessly. She already wanted to be gone but she visited her mother every week and stayed for exactly an hour. No matter how much she wanted to leave, she wouldn't leave a second before that. She owed her mother that much. She walked over to the kitchen table stacked with *US*, *People* and *OK!* Magazines and pushed them to the side. "I own dresses, Mom. On special occasions I even wear a few. But working ten-hour days in an office doesn't require fashion magazine attire. I wear what makes me comfortable. I'm comfortable in these." Kylie indicated her chained leggings.

"But the shoes, Kylie," her mother fussed. "Surely shoes that masculine and unattractive are not proper workplace attire. They don't look comfortable at all. In fact, they're very unattractive."

"Well, they're not, and I like them," Kylie defended her choice of attire even though she'd heard the argument a million times before. "I'll leave the spiked heels and frothy dresses to you." She left it unsaid that her mother's attire these days consisted of her bathrobe and slippers. The dresses and shoes stood unused and abandoned in her closet.

Kylie sat up straight, not touching the back of the chair. She knitted her fingers together and went through the ritual of visiting with her only relative.

"How's the job search going, Mom? Hear anything yet from those hair salons where you applied?"

Lana's mouth twisted into a frown. "Not yet. I was hopeful about the last one but, after the interview, they didn't call me back. I think the problem is that I'm not young anymore. All these salons want are hot, airhead stylists with fake boobs and spray tans. Those women can only do hair if the style requires mousse and gel. I'm a professional. I'm an artist! What I'm not is twenty-years-old. The beauty industry is a vain bitch."

While her mother had a point, Kylie thought her mother's appearance had a lot more to do with it than her age. The signs of dissipation were starting to show. She looked *worn*. As with everything, she wisely kept the observation to herself.

"Not that it matters anyway, sweetheart," Lana continued, thankfully not privy to her daughter's thoughts. "I'm doing alright. As you know, this is a Metro-Housing building so it's rent-controlled. My rent only goes up when my income does. The cost of living here has gone down considerably since the salon went under. I just keep my needs simple and the system takes good care of me."

Kylie got up and opened the fridge. There were cans of beer, bottles of wine, and wine coolers. There was very little food stacked on the shelves. "Mom, how about I give you some money for some essentials?" She offered although she already knew the answer. "I've stayed at this place longer than I've contracted anywhere else and they pay pretty well. I'm almost done paying off my student loan so I can afford to help. I'm doing well for myself these days."

"No, Kylie. We've talked about this. You gave me all the money you'd saved over the years to start up the salon. When Rodney ran off with the profits I swore I'd never take another dime that I didn't earn."

Kylie scowled at the mention of her mother's ex-boyfriend/business partner but wisely didn't comment as her mother continued, saying, "You've done enough for me. It's time for you to take care of yourself."

"I don't need much either," Kylie insisted. "The studio is adequate. It's in a good neighborhood. My clothing doesn't exactly require a steady infusion of cash. I save most of what I earn so I can afford to help you out."

"Helping me out is why that hefty student loan is still hanging over your head. You invested in the salon and my carelessness with men made that blow up in your face.

I'm so sorry, sweetie." Without warning, tears started to gather in Lana's eyes. "I still think about Rodney and how gullible I was. I don't know how you managed to forgive me. I'll pay you back, sweetie. I swear."

"Forget it, Mom. They'll catch up with Rodney soon enough. Hey, did I tell you that I have a new boss?" It was the only bit of news that Kylie could think of that would divert her mother's attention from the impending emotional breakdown.

"Is he cute?" Lana asked dabbing at her eyes with the hem of her nightgown.

"Um..." Kylie had to think about that. Not because her eyes hadn't registered Austin DeAngelis' physical appeal, but because she'd long ago grown immune to the flashy, slick-talking, playboy types. They reminded her too much of her absentee father. That alone was an instant buzz kill. "He's a very attractive man," she said finally. "Young though. A lot younger than I would have thought."

"Ohh, what's his name?" Her mother's tears instantly stopped. She hustled over to the crowded table and snatched up the unused paperweight, also known as the 7th generation iPad that Kylie had bought her last Christmas.

Kylie loved buying her mother technology almost as much as Lana loved not using it. Googling her new boss had finally given her mother use for the device that had a million other practical functions.

"Austin DeAngelis," Kylie said with an aggrieved sigh. She was already sorry she'd brought the topic up.

A squeal brought Kylie's head up. "Oh, he's gorgy," her mother exclaimed.

An unexpected laugh tumbled from Kylie's lips. "Gorgy? Meaning gorgeous? Mom, have you been watching old rap videos again?"

Her mother smirked. "I do love Drake. He's Canadian, you know."

"Yes, I know, Mom. But can we stop using phrases from rap songs in regular conversation? It's weird."

"Kylie, not everyone's music choices are as eclectic as yours. Plus, I must keep current so I can talk intelligently with the young misters and misses that plant their butts in my chair. Rap is the new rock. But enough of that, just look at this face!" She shoved the iPad under Kylie's nose.

Kylie found Austin DeAngelis staring back at her with dark-rimmed, aqua-colored eyes so light they seemed to almost glow. These disconcerting eyes were set against skin so darkly tanned that only some exotic ancestor could be blamed for its hue. He looked aggressively male, cultured, and refined. However, as if to thumb his nose at this impression, hair the color of new dimes was playfully and boyishly styled in an ultra-stylish faux-hawk. He looked rich, earthy, and dynamic. Even Kylie, who was immune to pretty faces, felt the online *Business Weekly* article seemed to come alive with his image peering out from it.

"Look at that hair!" Her mother exclaimed, forcing Kylie to study the picture of her boss. "Prematurely silver, isn't it?" She didn't wait for an answer. "I would kill to do that hair. Who does it? Do you know? Can you ask him? Maybe I can get an interview there. What I wouldn't do to have regular customers with hair like that."

"I have no idea who his stylist is, Mom. It's not like I can ask him. We're not exactly on a first-name basis."

"You could be," her mother shot back. Catching Kylie unaware, she snatched the clip from her daughter's hair, making the lush waves tumble down to the middle of her back. "You're a beautiful woman and I'm not just saying that because I'm your mother. You have your father's face. Not that mine is anything to sneeze at, especially in my younger days, but Soldier, for all his bad habits and faults, passed on some exceptional DNA. With the right clothes, you'd make some rich guy's heart stop."

Kylie carefully plucked the clip from her mother's fingers and twisted her hair back into its habitual top knot.

Soldier was what they called her recalcitrant father and her physical similarity to him was the last thing she wanted to discuss. Soldier had been visiting Canada on leave from the U.S. Army when her mother met him. Kylie was sure it was the uniform that made her mother fall so hard and so fast; that, and the fact that Soldier was a wordsmith. He knew how to charm anyone out of anything. In her mother's case, he'd charmed her onto her back long enough to make a child before he'd split.

Kylie had seen her father on and off throughout the years but never long enough to form a lasting relationship. It bothered her that she'd inherited anything from Soldier. It bothered her more that her mother never spoke badly of him although he abandoned her, leaving her with a child to raise. The fact that they were alone in the world, except for each other, made Kylie try hard to make the relationship with her mother work. She didn't have anyone else. Never had.

Chapter Three

Tim Horton's coffee in hand, with enough cream on top to cause cardiac arrest, Austin walked through the front doors of Avion and headed to his newly cleared office. It was so early that most of the hallway lights were still off. He flipped a switch and they flickered on as he made his way down the deserted corridor. Each time he bought or acquired a new company, he liked to get in early in the first few months of the acquisition so he could get a handle on how best to improve the company's bottom line. Avion had been in trouble right before he bought it. From what he could tell, it was mostly due to mismanagement and the Board not understanding their products' place in the marketplace.

Austin planned to change all that. He'd sent Brixton in as his right-hand man to take charge of things while he cleaned up another business deal in the Middle East. He was primed and ready to start Avion down the path to sales figures that were in the black. He was halfway to his office before he realized that at least one employee had made it to work before he had.

"Ms. Derringer-DeValle, what a surprise. Do we pay you to work from sunrise?" Austin asked amiably. Strolling into her cubicle, his presence instantly reduced its size.

Her head snapped up from what she was doing.

"Just Derringer," she said automatically, her chair swiveling in his direction. "Good morning, Mr. DeAngelis," she greeted him formally. "I'm a contractor, but I don't bill for the hours when I come in early. I'm paid from 8:00 a.m. but I do my best work while it's quiet."

"Well, I appreciate your dedication." He took a quick sip of his coffee. "And call me Austin, please. We don't stand on ceremony here. Can I call you Kylie?"

"If you must," she responded.

Austin's brow lifted at her reply.

"You're here early, aren't you?"

There was something in her tone that implied that he should be off sailing his yacht, drinking heavily in some swanky bar or debauching some blonde. Against his will, his lips tugged upward in a smile. Not the fake one he used to build rapport with his employees, but his real smile.

"I'm wounded, Madam." He gripped his heart. "I just bought this company. Where else would I be? You've read too many tabloids if you think I'd leave my company's health to anyone else. When I acquire something I want, I don't waste time putting my hands on it. I like to get my hands dirty."

Where did that come from? He hadn't intended to say that much but something about the boldness in her gaze, the way she was subtly leaning toward him, spurred him on. "What about you? No social life? I'll weep for the entire male population if you tell me you're married to your work."

She laughed and then frowned as if she hadn't intended to do that. "I'm not married to it, but I like what I do. Writing is hard but technical writing requires discipline and attention to detail. I like the preciseness. I like that there's not a lot of room for spontaneity."

The answer surprised him. His gaze slid over her. "You don't approve of spontaneity, Kylie? Don't you ever take risks? Break the rules?"

"Not lately," she murmured then stiffened and spun around to face her computer. His eyebrows hiked when she started typing as if forgetting him.

That wouldn't do. Gripping her chair firmly, he turned her back to face him and let his seriousness show in his gaze. "Don't do that. It's rude. We weren't finished talking and I don't like being dismissed."

Was he imagining the way her breathing hitched? Or the flash of fire in her eyes? She lifted her head.

"Was there something else you wanted to discuss, sir? I thought you came in early so you could work. I know I did."

Challenge accepted. His lips quirked and he stepped away from her chair. "Of course. I apologize for talking your ear off. Just getting to know my new employee. I've learned a lot. I'll leave you to your work."

Turning, he strode down the hall to his office. Seated at his desk, he stared blankly at the computer screen.

Screw it. He picked up the phone and dialed her number, ignoring that he already had her extension memorized. "Ms. DeValle. A moment in my office please."

He disconnected before she could reply, knowing that would irritate her. He chuckled. This was going to be fun.

"Ms. DeValle," Austin greeted when she strode into his office.

"Ms. Derringer," she repeated. "I don't use the second surname."

"Yeah, right. I forgot. Please take a seat." Austin sat back at his desk and then proceeded to stare at her without speaking as she lowered herself into one of the ultra-modern chairs that decorated his office.

***

Uncomfortable under his gaze, Kylie looked around. His office had been redecorated weeks before Austin had shown up. When she'd seen all that European styled furniture being unloaded from the freight elevator, she'd made some assumptions about what type of man her new boss was going to be. Every piece of furniture was metallic, aggressively unconventional, minimalistic in its beauty, and visibly expensive. Design that imaginative didn't come cheap. The chair she sat on was of some metal mesh material curved into the shape of an S. It shouldn't have been comfortable, but it was. That made up for the fact that, as far as chairs went, the one she was in was intimidating.

Kylie gave her boss her full attention, waiting patiently for him to begin speaking. He didn't right away. Instead, he seemed content to study her in silence. Kylie fought the urge to fidget. She wasn't naturally patient. The air of quiet composure was a trait she'd worked hard to cultivate. She'd learned that impatience and haste always had awful consequences, so she waited.

Austin's eyes roamed over her attire, taking in the black wool cardigan with big metal buttons that she'd paired with black tights and knee-high riding boots with a gold metal plate at the heel. Through his eyes, she probably resembled a slightly Goth riding instructor. For some reason, Kylie wished she'd worn something that matched his charcoal grey business suit, white shirt, and the pink tie streaked with grey. The ensemble could have been effeminate but wasn't. She felt like a preschooler who'd played dress up in her mother's closet. She frowned at the thought.

"What's on your mind, Kylie?"

Kylie sat up straighter. "Just wondering what I can do for you, sir. I have tons of work on my desk."

"*Sir?*" Austin raised an eyebrow at her formality. "Why don't you let me worry about the work on your desk for now," he said. "Tell me a little bit about yourself — your background and your experience. What brought you to Avion and why haven't we been able to lure you into becoming a permanent employee?"

Kylie's frown deepened. She imagined she looked like a cherub in a snit. Smoothing away the frown with effort, she said, "All that information is in my HR file. Am I being interviewed again?" she asked, holding his gaze. "I'm happy to indulge you but it'll be quicker for you just to read through my file."

Austin leaned back in his chair. "Prickly."

"I beg your pardon?"

"You're prickly," he repeated. "Why is that?"

"I'm not prickly," Kylie denied through gritted teeth. "I'm just not used to being called into my boss's office for a private sit-down when the HR manager can tell him anything he wants to know."

"Despite what you may think, I called you into my office for a reason. That reason has nothing to do with the fact that you're pretty. That's it, right? You're suspicious of men playing games or using power to get your attention. You're used to rebuffing their advances with your wintery personality. Let me put your mind to rest Ms. DeValle, while you obviously have an attractive package, you're not my type. Now that we've cleared up the notion that I've called you into my office to persuade you to lay naked across my desk, can we get back to my original query?"

"Ms. Derringer," Kylie said automatically.

"What?" Austin asked, his brow knitting.

"You called me, Ms. DeValle. I've said before that I don't use the second surname."

"Yes, that's right. Why don't we start with that?" Austin said, his attention on her face. "Why do you have a second surname if you don't want people using it?"

Kylie felt her shoulders bunch. Rebellion and resentment were building in her chest, but she fought against the emotions. She counted to ten and then fifteen before even attempting to speak, taking a calming breath before she began. "I'm in the process of having the second surname legally removed. I just haven't gotten around to it.

Derringer is my mother's maiden name. I'm estranged from my father so the name DeValle has never felt right. When I was young I had no recourse to make changes, but now that I am older, I've decided to make the switch permanently." She looked directly at him. "Are you satisfied?"

Austin's mouth kicked up. "I doubt you could satisfy me Kylie, but the explanation was good enough." His mouth hitched up further when she let out a sound resembling a hiss. "Now, the reason you're here." Austin leaned back further in his chair, all evidence of playfulness leaving his face. "As you may have heard, I create and design things. My talent is in buying companies that can build the things I imagine. Recently, I've thought up something new. I usually wouldn't discuss a project this important with a contractor, but I've heard nothing but good things about your work. I don't want to run the risk of hiring someone from the outside when I have someone capable of doing the job right here. I have a highly sensitive project in mind. It's going to require that you consider signing on full-time here as an Avion employee. You'll have to sign non-disclosure and non-compete agreements; it will also require that you work closely with me and a few high-level employees."

Kylie started to shake her head, but Austin held up his hand. "Before you decide to forego the opportunity completely, let me explain a few things. I want to stress the fact that the job comes with a hefty pay increase, but something tells me that won't appeal to you. Instead, I'll tell you that the project we're working on will have a huge impact on the marketplace. Describing the benefits of my project will challenge every writing skill you've ever had. You'll be at the forefront of some revolutionary stuff. How the world understands our product, how it's perceived and used, will largely rest with you. We want the user experience to be multidimensional. The plan is to move beyond the user's manual into more innovative applications. Of course, understanding how you work best, we would make every effort to give you the autonomy you need to excel."

That intrigued her. "Tell me more."

"Avion's chief competitor is a company called Sempia," he began enthusiastically. "Sempia is in the business of creating financial software that aids traders in making deals over the internet. For the last few years, Avion has unsuccessfully been trying to compete with their highly successful product Oasis. To explain it in the simplest terms possible, Avion, under my direction, will be creating and launching new software that will revolutionize how traders make money. My algorithm and its soon-to-be software are highly confidential. I bought this company to make my product a reality. I'm assembling the best internal team possible to bring it to the marketplace. I need your help."

"Why me?" Kylie asked, her lips curled in cynicism.

Austin smiled, leaned back, and crossed his hands over his stomach. Her gaze was drawn to his taut stomach, which didn't seem to have a hint of extra flesh.

"Cynical much?"

"I beg your pardon?"

"Kylie, let's clear something up," Austin held her gaze. "You're a beautiful woman. From all accounts, maybe this fact has in some way made your life difficult — men coming on to you, unwanted attention, and perhaps some borderline sexual harassment." He held his hand up when she started to speak. "But please, let me be clear. Like any red-blooded male, I have taken note of your attractiveness, but that in no way affects my business decisions."

"Without conceit," he continued, "I'd also like to add that I own sixteen companies, my net worth is substantial, and well, just look at me," he said waving his hands in front of his face. "I've been the subject of interest of beautiful women like yourself before. I don't hit on unwilling or unavailable women. I don't promote them in the hopes of a friendly fuck in my California King. I have businesses to run and I run those businesses with aggressiveness and ferocity. I sensed that same kind of ferociousness in you and that's why we're here. If you want to sleep with me, I accept. If you don't, can we get back to business, please?"

"You're very blunt." Kylie was impressed.

"I thought you'd appreciate it," he said.

"I do," she admitted. "Please continue. You have my full attention."

"At last."

Kylie's mouth drew up into something resembling a smile. Austin relaxed, leaned back in his chair and ran his hands through his high sheen steel-colored hair.

Kylie shifted in her chair. She wondered if it should bother her that she instantly wondered how precisely his hair must be cut that his hands running through it failed to alter its shape? His hair must be as perfect as when he left the house that morning. Being the daughter of a hairdresser, she noticed these things. She noticed that there was only the barest hint of black among the silver. He must have started going grey very young.

"...Your Masters and undergraduate degrees in English combined with your minor in Computer Science make you ideal for this position."

Kylie focused on his mouth as he said the words. She tried to focus on what he was saying but other thoughts kept filling her head. Like what did that hair look like wet from a shower, the owner wet and dripping with just a scanty towel covering his hips? The hair, was there enough of it for a woman's hands to grab hold of it and pull? She was appalled by these thoughts but couldn't stop them. He was her boss. Correction. He was her boss's boss. She had no right to think about him in that way. She didn't want him. Since her breakup with Kory, she hadn't even looked at a man. But there she was with vivid, highly explicit thoughts of her employer running through her head. What was wrong with her? She couldn't even begin to speculate.

"The answer is yes, I take it?" Austin's question interrupted her thoughts.

Kylie blinked and brought her thoughts under control. "Yes, to what? The job? I'll have to think about it. Can I have a few days? I enjoy my autonomy and I'm not sure a permanent job is worth it for any reason, even for something as exciting as what you've described. If the timeline is crucial, and you need an answer right away, then I'll have to pass."

"No, Derringer."

The way he said her name, last name only, sent a shiver up her spine.

"Your part of the project would become important once we've completed the project and gone through all the initial testing phases," Austin explained. He was oblivious to her preoccupation. "You can have some time, but that's not what I was talking about. I asked you earlier if you

34

wanted to sleep with me. By the way you're looking at me, can I assume the answer is yes?"

"No!" Kylie said feeling a dark flush stealing over cheeks and spreading across her chest. "The answer is definitely *no* to that." She was mortified.

"Really?" he challenged, giving her a look that must had gotten more than one woman's panties wet. "I have enough experience to know when a woman wants me, and you do."

"God, you're arrogant," she said helplessly impressed by his confidence despite herself.

"Does arrogance do it for you, Kylie? I can show you more if it does."

"You're incredible," she said. Unexpected and highly inappropriate laughter bubbled up in her chest.

"In more ways than one," he agreed without a hint of sarcasm.

Kylie's eyes flicked down the length of him in a quick sensual assessment. Yes, he would be incredible, wouldn't he? Her eyes lingered over the mound his zipper concealed. Before her eyes, the mound grew impressively. When she looked up, startled, Austin's expression was rueful.

"An unruly bugger, isn't he? I thought I had him trained well enough to only respond to direct stimulation and not to leap to attention at the slightest provocation. Here he goes embarrassing me. He seems to like you a lot."

35

Kylie got a hold of herself. "He might like me but any kind of interaction in that direction is out of the question."

Austin studied her closely, his face revealing nothing. "You're probably right." He conceded easily, too easily if she was honest. "An affair with me would be difficult for you — in more ways than one."

Alone later in her apartment, Kyle wondered what he meant. She was not an inexperienced woman. Not in the bedroom, boardroom, or any room Austin could think of. She knew how to handle herself. Her sexual experience wasn't extensive, but she was a perfectionist. Anything she did she made sure she did it well. Making love was no exception. She liked exceeding expectations, so when her boyfriend in college introduced her to the mysteries of sex, after the first awkward moments, she set her mind to mastering the intricacies of making love.

At first, she was preoccupied with pleasing her partners. She focused on knowing just where to touch, how to move, what to lick, and when and how hard to bite. Later, when she felt she had mastery over the male anatomy and had identified all their pleasure points, she turned her mind to figuring out how to please herself. She knew what she liked. She knew what men liked and there was very little in the bedroom that was off-limits for her. It was the one place that she let herself be free.

There, she was expressive, inventive, and uninhibited. She let loose the bounds that governed her life and enjoyed the careless freedom that came with sex. A profligate playboy Austin might be, but *she* was a student of pleasure. If she was ever reckless enough to even contemplate Austin as a lover, he would be the one unprepared. With the wicked thought upper-most in her mind, Kylie dressed for bed, lay down, closed her eyes, and teased herself with visions of all the things she knew how to do to bring a man like Austin DeAngelis to his knees.

Chapter Four

O ver the next few weeks, Kylie got used to seeing Austin's titanium head around the office. He was always in constant motion. Someone who was legendary for her ability to give her complete attention to any project to which she was assigned, found herself looking up throughout the day just to watch his movements. He was tireless. He left the day-to-day running of the business to Brixton and instead seemed to spend most of his time ensconced in meetings with the Tech Team. They'd be at it for hours — a select and chosen group of Avion staff members. Everyone else's day remained the same, but Austin had something he wanted from the group. Something he was passionate enough about to direct himself. It wasn't long after his arrival at the company that the lawyers came. A small army of them loaded with briefcases stuffed with legal looking papers. The rumor was that *the chosen ones* were handpicked to work on the new boss's special project and, as such, were required to sign non-disclosure agreements. Every meeting after the lawyers came was secret, for a select few. Papers in the trash were shredded after every meeting, whiteboards wiped clean, and lips sealed tight. No one seemed to mind the change in the office.

No one except her.

For everyone outside of the elite circle, life and work went on as usual. Kylie was consumed with the need to know. So, it wasn't long before she found herself mingling ever so slightly with the Tech team doing the unthinkable — talking to her co-workers. All but a few were startled by her new friendliness but were happy to talk and gossip with her if she kept the topic away from anything to do with Austin and his new project. The mere mention of the topic made gregarious and naturally loquacious men turn mute, taciturn.

She was dying to be involved, but it was her own damn fault that she was on the outside looking in. She'd turned down the opportunity and blown the chance to work on something that had the geeks in the office walking around with their cheeks flushed. They were excited and their excitement made her envious. She enjoyed a challenge, and the project was surely the most challenging thing to roll through Avion's doors in months. She wanted in. She was too proud to reconsider the offer Austin had extended to her, especially since their last inappropriate conversation in his office, he hadn't looked at her or spoken to her again. She was another underling, just another employee. If she wasn't on the team, she didn't matter.

Austin couldn't keep his eyes to himself. Was he obsessed? he wondered. How else could he explain why his employee occupied every corner of his thoughts that wasn't filled with the plans for his product launch? He was obsessed with bringing the new product to the marketplace but found he was more than a little preoccupied with Kylie. What was it about her? She was beautiful, yes, but in his world, beauty was commonplace. Yes, she was lush and had generous curves in all the right places that would enthrall any man. But she was so *tiny*. He didn't do tiny women.

Austin wasn't the kind of man that liked inflicting pain on the opposite sex. There were men who liked their women childlike and androgynous for obvious reasons, but he wasn't one of them. He usually liked his women leggy, long, and fit. He felt like a giant beside Kylie, and that should have turned him off. Instead, it turned him on. In her eyes was the promise of being able to take whatever he had to offer. The thought was ridiculous. Most women couldn't manage the size and girth of him, and he'd learned through the years

41

that, for him, restraint, patience, and self-control were what made sex possible with most women. Why then did he have visions of ravaging Kylie Derringer no second surname? Why did he think that between her thighs promised ecstasy and pleasure he could only dream about? He wanted her. He spent his time plotting how to get her in bed even as he dismissed those thoughts as soon as they occurred. He couldn't sleep with an employee. It was bad for business. But he wanted to sleep with her. He longed to spend hours between her thighs with his dick buried deep and his tongue tasting every inch of her.

Unlike him, his father liked hurting women — physically. He enjoyed hurting his mother most of all. As she was his wife and obligated by marriage to endure him, theirs was not a union based on anything as *provincial* as love. Love didn't factor into the DeAngelis household. It was no wonder then that he knew nothing of the emotion personally.

Except for his grandfather, Austin didn't have good role models. He would have willingly loved his mother and been a comfort to her if she'd let him, but Brinkley DeAngelis wasn't interested in any warmth or affection from her son. To her, he was collateral and she used him as such to get her way with her husband. She'd produced him to secure her part of her husband's large fortune, and once she had done that, she had lost all interest in the role of being a mother. She'd fobbed him off on nannies and spent only the barest amount of time with him when he was growing up. Not knowing a mother's love hadn't stopped him from yearning for it. He'd tried to gain his mother's affection and attention by any means that were available to him.

All his efforts had failed.

It had taken Austin his entire childhood to understand that his mother's unhappy marriage wasn't the reason for her iciness. Her husband's need to dominate her in and out of the bedroom only played the smallest part in her coldness and detachment. Brinkley had come to the marriage already encased in ice. Her husband's treatment had only caused the winter to spread. She loved fine clothes, exquisite jewelry, and luxury trips. Those were the things that made her happy. They made the sacrifice of having to contend with her husband's demands and her son's petulance worthwhile. The two men in her life were nuisances she learned to bear. One she endured and the other she ignored.

So, no, he couldn't have Kylie hard and fast against a wall. He couldn't ram into her with fervor as she lay on the floor naked and ready for him. Couldn't rip her clothes from her body and let his dick dance inside of her until she screamed, until he screamed; until they both screamed —

their voices raspy and raw from the vocalization of their pleasure. The situation was impossible.

"Have dinner with me." Austin heard himself asking Kylie out but couldn't believe his own ears. *What the fuck?* When he walked up to her cubicle, it was the last thing he expected to come out of his mouth. Thank God she sat away from everyone else, because if anyone overheard his invitation, his reputation would be in shreds — his humiliation complete.

She looked at him with those solemn grey eyes, swallowed visibly, and looked away from him before she answered. "I can't, you know that. It's inappropriate for you to ask me." The words were a reprimand.

"Of course, it's inappropriate," Austin agreed. "It's also unprofessional and highly improper on my part, but I don't give a fuck. Have dinner with me." Now that he'd committed to asking her, his determination grew. She would say yes. She just didn't know it yet.

"No," she repeated, her eyes roaming over him in a way that told him she wanted to give him a more affirmative answer.

"Tell me why?" He could hear the aggression in his voice. It made the question a command.

She started to speak but he held his hand up. "Don't give me any of the bullshit reasons I gave you. Give me one good reason besides me being your boss why you can't."

"Because you don't want dinner. You want something else." She was biting her lip.

Fuck, she was right. He stared at her without comment and let his aqua eyes speak. His gaze parted her shirt and touched her breasts. It opened and unzipped her pants and let the tip, just the tip, of his finger slip into her wet center. His hands then spanned her waist, picked her up and rested her heat against the part of him that wanted to be inside. His eyes told her the truth so he didn't bother to lie. "You're right. I don't want dinner. I do want to eat something though. Let me."

Jesus Christ! Kylie's brain flat-lined. Was he fucking kidding? Who could say no to words so blunt, raw, and direct? No platitudes. No lies. No dissembling. Kory, her ex, was all about lies, misdirection, and half-truths. Her father was the same way. She barely knew Austin but already she respected that he didn't play games. He asked for what he wanted without apology. He was unrelenting and unapologetic. It turned her on. But fucking her boss wasn't a good idea. Or was it? Dating her boss wasn't a good idea.

Austin was the kind of man that loved them and left them. She could tell. Except for her stint with Kory when she thought a relationship was what she wanted, she was the same. No love and expectations, then no heartbreak. It was all so tempting.

The truth was that she liked discipline. Adored it. She loved routine, convention, rigidity, and self-control. She excelled at control over herself and didn't make a move without thoroughly thinking through the outcome. She analyzed everything, tested, and weighed her decisions using intellect instead of her heart. That was the only way she'd been able to survive her teenage years and her chaotic home life.

But she harbored a secret, a secret she admitted only to herself. Deep down she knew a lack of diligence on her part would result in her wild and impetuous side taking over. Deep at her core, she longed for adventure, carnality, and vice. She had a reckless side to her nature that she hungered to explore. In the end though, she didn't dare. Couldn't risk it. Could she? She'd seen firsthand what letting one's emotions rule led to and she wasn't going to fall into that trap. For now, and for the foreseeable future, she was staid Kylie Derringer and she planned to stay that way even if Austin was temptation itself. Even if her every waking moment centered on tasting, touching, and licking every inch of his delectable skin.

His gaze held hers. With his gaze alone, Austin promised to satisfy her every craving. His gaze promised to make her lapse in judgment worth her while. Fuck it; they were adults; they could establish upfront that there would be no commitment except a commitment to their own self-interests. She knew she was inventing reasons to be bad, but she didn't care. She'd been good for far too long anyway.

"Where do you live?"

Austin blinked. Then his eyes narrowed and his nostrils flared. "East Liberty."

"Really? I pictured you as a heart-of-the-city, downtown Toronto man. No matter. I get off at 5 p.m. I can be at your place by 6. No dinner, just a good time, and then we go back to our lives like this never happened. Agreed?"

"Agreed," Austin said smoothly and with lightning speed. Unobtrusively, he slid his personal business card with his address across her desk and walked away. He didn't bother to look back. Kylie stared after him. What the hell had she just done? But it was too late to back out. She was committed.

The ding of the opening elevator startled Kylie. All through what was left of her workday, she'd alternately been daydreaming or silently freaking out. As soon as she'd pulled up at the address Austin had given her, she'd felt like throwing up, felt like jamming her foot on the gas of her Hyundai and driving away as fast as she could. She'd looked up at the glass building that seemed to touch the sky and stared at the parking valet like he was royalty when he'd approached her. He'd plucked the keys from her numb fingers with a half-grin on his face.

Kylie didn't pretend that she'd grown up anywhere else except low-income housing. She was self-made, and proud of it, but pretending she was beyond being impressed was ludicrous. She'd never seen wealth on this scale. Half-dazed, she wandered into the lobby. That was another ordeal. The concierge at the front desk made her knees knock with his sophistication and his quiet efficiency. She didn't intimidate easily but Austin's lobby had more elegance than she'd ever seen outside of HGTV's *Extreme Homes*. The elevator doors dinged again and threatened to close with her still in it. Startled, she leaped out and into a living room the size of a small football field.

"Welcome to my home, Kylie. I'm glad you came." With bare feet, V-neck t-shirt and jeans that rode low on lean hips, Austin seemed to glide towards her. She watched him, transfixed, as he came up to her and lightly kissed her cheek. Her flesh burned in the spot his mouth touched. At that moment, she knew that she was in trouble and as over her head as she'd ever been. So, she did what she did best — she retreated. *Shields up*, she told herself silently and envisioned the imaginary emotional wall rising around her. She could do this.

Giving her host a half-smile, she left his side and wandered over to the panoramic floor to ceiling windows that wrapped around the entire penthouse. She gazed out at views that touched prominent Toronto landmarks like the CN Tower. Everything was right there. It was simply breathtaking.

"Nice view," she commented, turning back in his direction.

He smiled showing all his teeth, seeming genuinely amused. "Well, thank you. Can I offer you something to eat? Maybe something to drink? Champagne? Wine? I can give you a tour if you like." He offered a reprieve. He was possibly working hard to make her comfortable, trying to melt some of the ice that had come over her. It was all in vain though. She wanted one thing from Austin and he didn't have to feed her first to get it.

"Let's start with the tour," she said, removing her jacket. She'd come in her work clothes. She hadn't had the time or the inclination to change. Who was she trying to impress anyway?

"No problem," he said, his eyes never leaving her face. "Well, the penthouse has five bedrooms and is roughly 3000 square feet," he began. "I have the full upper floor on three levels. No neighbors. There's plenty to see but I think I'll take you to see the inside pool first. Care for a quick swim? The rest of the apartment can wait until later if you do."

Kylie listened to him talk but mostly she just watched his mouth moving. He had a beautiful mouth. Realizing she hadn't answered his question about the swim, she took off her four-inch wedge shoes and placed them neatly against the beautiful black leather Italian sofa. She then pulled her top over her head to expose her pink lace bra. Austin stopped speaking. She unzipped her pants and dragged them down her legs and stepped out of them to expose hot pink high-waisted boy shorts that showed more of her figure than it hid. She was all-girl when it came to her undergarments. Her mother would be so proud. She pulled her hair from its top knot and let the luxurious waves fall down her back.

"Can I swim in these?" She fingered the pink lace.

"Beautiful," he said with a sigh. "Petite. Lush. I knew there was a body underneath all those clothes, but my imagination didn't do you justice. You're more beautiful than I ever dreamed." Austin shook himself. "Do you still want to swim? I have other ways of making you wet," he said gruffly.

"I do." Kylie strode past him so that her assets were on full display. She glanced over her shoulder at him under half-lowered eyelids. "The pool is in this palace of yours somewhere, I presume? I'll find it myself," she said, walking away. "When I'm done with my swim, I want a tour of your bedroom, your bedsheets, and what is inside those jeans. Agreed?"

Austin swallowed. "Agreed."

Chapter Five

Austin was jealous. He was jealous of a man he'd never met. He was jealous of an artist no less. An artist who probably had piercings everywhere: in his ears, lips, and septum. Unlike him, the dude wouldn't be well-groomed but unkempt with clothes that looked lived in. Unlike his perfectly styled hair, he imagined the object of his ire had a partially shaved head with multicolored strands standing on end in gelled tufts.

The man he wanted to hurt made a living using his hands and the money he earned was never enough to stretch from one day to the next. Austin had several homes but the guy that made him envious and angry possibly shared an apartment with friends. He probably never left the area he was born in.

Despite that, Austin was jealous. He was jealous because that same man had had the privilege of touching and caressing Kylie's skin before him. He'd crouched over her and pressed his instrument into her flesh repeatedly causing her pain, but the kind of pain she liked; the kind of pain that left lasting marks. If he was good, she would always remember his touch; always remember how it felt for him to be a permanent part of her flesh and her history. Every time she was naked and saw herself in the mirror, she would remember him. Every time she touched herself, she would recall his expert hands and his skilled touch. Austin wanted to hurt this unknown man even as he admired the beauty he'd created with his talented fingers.

Kylie stood in front of him almost as naked as she'd been earlier, except she'd used her hands to lower the waistband of her lace boy shorts so that the briefs rode extra low on her hips. That's when he'd seen it and had nearly lost his mind. In his past, he'd seen many women naked and he'd admired their milky-white, brown, and black limbs devoid of spots, bruises, or blemishes of any kind. Back then, he'd been certain that he liked his women unmarked, perfect and pristine, smooth and unspoiled in any way, but he was wrong. He liked his women inked. Even as he hated the tattoo artist who'd given Kylie her permanent ink, his eyes and his cock loved the results. Two small and intricately designed Derringer pistols decorated Kylie's flawless body. The artist had taken such care with the design that the guns looked lifelike and ready to shoot. Any man who saw the tattoos on Kylie would be ready to shoot as well.

Placed anywhere on her body the guns would have been erotic, both a warning of danger and a lure, but the placement of the firearms inspired lust. The short barrels of the guns were out of sight, pointing down to a place on Kylie's anatomy that Austin wanted to bury his face in. One on each side, the handles of the pistols stuck out at the edge of her panties, beckoning him to come closer to study the design. The guns lured the unsuspecting to danger. Who in their right mind would care about protecting themselves when putting their head and lips between two guns shielding such a prize? He wanted the guns pointing at him. He wanted to see them quiver when the owner got trigger happy and begged for release. He wanted to be in the middle of a gunfight with his hands and tongue firmly on the trigger.

Kylie gave him a knowing look and jumped, feet-first, into the pool. She swam leisurely up and down the length of the pool, seemingly oblivious to the fully clothed man watching her. She didn't beckon him in. He realized then that she didn't require his presence in the water to enjoy herself. She was a nymph. She was a sensual creature with the water all around her. She floated on her back, her breasts bobbing temptingly just above the surface.

Austin felt his throat go dry. He ran a hand down the front of his erection to calm the tension inside of him. *Whoa, boy,* he whispered to himself. He sat down in a chair by the edge of the pool and watched Kylie as she tormented him. Did she know what she was doing to him? Did she have any idea how much trouble she was in if he didn't calm down? Already his heart was racing in his chest. Had he ever wanted a woman this bad? No.

Eventually, she came out of the pool and approached him smiling. "Thanks for that. I love the water but, as you can imagine, my lifestyle doesn't allow me a lot of time to indulge."

"No problem. My..." He coughed and tried the words again not liking how gruff and needy they sounded coming out of his mouth. "My pleasure, Kylie. My pool is yours to use anytime you wish. I'll tell the downstairs concierge to allow you access."

"Thank you, Austin. That's very generous of you. Now that I'm relaxed and happy, a rare occurrence I assure you." She laughed at herself. "Shall we go and see what your shower and bed look like?"

"Yes." It was the only word Austin could manage to say coherently. This little girl was making him sweat. He shouldn't refer to her that way. He'd seen her partially naked. She was *all* woman.

Stripped down to a pair of white boxer briefs, he stood in his large bedroom. To his left, his neatly made king-sized bed mocked him. He wanted to dirty the sheets. He stared out the window, one arm on the ledge, the other hand on his slightly bent head with his fingers gripping his silver hair in agitation. Intently, he listened to the faint sound of the shower running in the bathroom. She had unerringly picked his bedroom from the three others on this level.

Currently, she was making use of his shower. He pictured the water running down her body, between her breast and pooling in the juncture of her thighs. Did the water tangle in a triangle of velvet fleece? Did it run smoothly unencumbered by anything except the angles of smooth petal-soft skin? Thinking about it, he shuddered. Would she come out wrapped in one of his fluffy white towels? Would she take the time to put the hot pink underwear back on for effect?

Austin's hand tightened in his hair and he groaned. He should have warned her. He looked down at his erection already threatening to tear a hole in the cotton of his briefs and thought she would take one look at him and change her mind. If he could get the tip of his cock into her without her crying out for him to stop, he'd be damn lucky. Preparing her to receive even that much of him would take forever.

Perspiration dotted his brow in anticipation. His proportions always came as a shock, not always a pleasant one, when ladies in his life got their first good look at him. *I should have warned her*. He usually did before he got to this stage, but Kylie had caught him by surprise.

He gripped himself and rubbed his large hand over the head of his penis, trying to ease some of the awful anticipation coursing through his body. What was wrong with him? He'd never felt this way before. There was no accounting for his hunger. He already knew the outcome would be disastrous but just the thought of Kylie's tight walls covering his erection made him want to come. Maybe he should start without her. More than likely, he would end without her anyway when she saw what awaited her.

He caught sight of her. Her hair was wet. Everything was wet! Good God! She'd forgone the towel and the underwear and come out naked. On dainty but damp feet, she walked up to him, stood on her tiptoes, and raised her head for a kiss. No shyness and no hesitation. Austin's tongue swept into her mouth. He picked her up and dragged her small body against him and wrapped her surprisingly long legs around his waist. He placed her high, above his belly button, so she wouldn't feel the strength of him and be afraid.

He then proceeded to kiss her hungrily and she responded in kind with an enthusiasm that left him breathless. *Calm down!* he shouted to himself. He stiffened another two inches. She was already in trouble, and her boldness was only making it worse.

"Let me feel you," she mumbled into his mouth, sucking his tongue with long and deep strokes.

Austin almost lowered her instinctively. "Not yet. I want to talk to you." He said the words, but was that his voice that sounded so shaky? He would have felt embarrassed if he wasn't so desperate.

She lowered her arms to feel between them. "Let's talk after."

"Wait!" he stopped her, lifting her high in half-panic. "We really need to talk."

She leaned back in his arms and looked at him with irritation. "Talk. Fast."

Austin looked at the storm clouds gathering in her eyes and the obstinate set of her jaw. He knew from his interactions with her that words would never have any impact on a woman this naturally stubborn. He set her down on the floor in front of him. When she was on her feet, he stepped back and without any other words, dragged his boxers down his legs and stepped out of them. He stood with his legs apart and his stance wide. He knew what he looked like with his shaft rising way past his navel. Every inch of him from base to tip was thick, pulsing, and hungry.

The silence was deafening. Kylie's gaze was riveted to his cock, and it was torturous. At any moment he expected her to grab her clothes and run. Instead, she said nothing. Did nothing. She stared, her eyes roaming over him, calculating, assessing, and caressing.

Austin couldn't take it anymore. "Say something, dammit!"

She remained quiet.

Frustrated and angry, even though he'd gone through this same scenario with countless women a million times before, he swung away from her and bent to pick up his boxers. Her words froze him.

"Do you know how to use that thing? Please, tell me that you do. It will be the greatest tragedy of my life to see something that magnificent up close with no functional use."

"I know exactly how to use it," Austin said on a growl. Perspiration dotted his brow, irritation making his words come out low and thick.

"We'll see," Kylie said calmly. She then turned away from him, walked over to the bed, threw the comforter to the floor, and lay down naked on the eight hundred thread count Egyptian cotton sheets. She turned her head to look at him with flashes of excitement and expectation. "Ready when you are."

Austin groaned as his balls tightened. She was unintimidated, ready, and willing. He released the death grip he had on the condom in his hand and sheathed himself with speed and efficiency. He already wanted to come.

"Jesus Christ." Sweat broke out on Austin's forehead. Her pussy was like a vice, squeezing him in the most delicious ways. Austin battled the urge to thrust up and in — hard, in one fluid movement that would satisfy his need for aggression. He kept himself strictly under control — but barely. He wanted to ram into her without consideration for anything but his own pleasure. He wanted to wrap her legs around his back, grip her hair, bury his face in her neck and let the animal in him have its way, plundering, pushing, and thrusting as he sought that place in her that would make him forget the years of deprivation and seemingly endless restraint.

Austin shook with the effort it took him to be what he'd taught himself to be: gentle, solicitous, and careful. Kylie brought out the worst in him. She made him want to break things. Rules. Boundaries. Barriers. He tried to hang on to his vow to treat women like precious glass. But dear God, Kyle seemed to like a little pain, seemed to like it a lot. She wasn't about to shatter. No, instead she gripped his buttocks hard and pressed down with force, jacking him into her body another agonizing inch. Her breath hitched in excitement and she repeated the action pushing him higher and further into her until he felt the sensual dew of her pleasure coat his dick making it possible for him to slam into her full force and to the hilt. He groaned, loud and deep as his pleasure reached its zenith. The sound was no competition for Kylie's scream. But it was a good scream. A scream of pleasure. Austin thrust once, hard and forceful, drew back and thrust again like he'd never been able to do before. Like he wanted, all out and without restraint; the sensation was too good, his body jerked as an unexpected orgasm took him. He emptied himself into her, giving her everything he had in him. The convulsions went on and on tightening everything inside of him. His balls drew up, his scalp tightened, his muscles tensed. Pleasure as he had never known rocked through him in an explosion of bright lights behind his closed eyelids. He was finished. Done. He was ruined for any other woman. His body shook, shuddered once more, and then everything went black in his mind as contentment clothed his body in quiet bliss. Her voice shattered the moment.

"Is that it then? I was expecting more," she said, shaking her head in clear disappointment. "Don't worry about it though; it was fun while it lasted. At least one of us is satisfied. I'm gonna go. Later." She made a move to shift from beneath him and off the bed. Everything in Austin rebelled and blazed back to life. Seconds ago, he would have bet his life's savings that he had no more energy left. That pleasure so profound and unexpected had drained him. But just a few callous words, thrown out in an oblique challenge, had him roaring back to life. His body responded to the insult of his masculinity with the appearance of a hard, solid erection that had scared women greater than Kylie Derringer into stuttering silence. His bed partner didn't bat an eye. She clenched her walls around his erection, looked at him, and shrugged.

"Yes, it feels impressive but when someone purchases a racehorse one does so with the promise of a good, hard ride. I need a thoroughbred Mr. DeAngelis. If you're not up to the challenge, then let's just quit while we're ahead."

Austin sat up wordlessly, muscles rippling as he moved with sweat dripping into the indentions on his stomach where muscle met bone. He dislodged from her, grabbed another condom from the bedside table, and sheathed himself before he scooped her up with one hand, and walked with her over to his couch. He sat and dropped her onto his lap. Her legs dangled off his knees seeming yards away from the ground as he placed her sideways on his naked limbs. He lifted her partially up and touched her clit with blunt fingertips. Kylie jumped in surprise and then exhaled in pleasure as Austin increased the pressure and the friction. In and out his hands moved. They were swift and sure, knowing where and how to touch her. In seconds, he built her back into a wild frenzy.

"Yes, Austin, yes," she panted. "Just like that. Don't stop." Her head fell sideways onto his shoulder and she squeezed her eyes shut as the pleasure built. Austin found one distended nipple with his tongue, sucking hard and fast. He wasn't gentle, and she liked it. He gorged himself on her breast like a man who was starved and she was his means of sustenance. Her body started to sing and vibrate as the pleasure built.

"More, I want more. Give me more, dammit." Kylie slapped his shoulder in frustration when he released her breast from his mouth with an audible pop. He wasn't finished with her, however. He gauged her readiness by touching her between her legs. Her pleasure soaked his fingers. Austin worked her, pushing one and then two fingers into her, moving fast and vigorously until Kylie was almost weeping with ecstasy.

She was cresting, shudders racking her small body when abruptly Austin pulled his fingers from her sheath. The shock of losing him made Kylie sit up straight in his lap and focus all her attention on him. Their eyes battled each other for short moments before Austin's long lashes swept down to cover his eyes. When he looked at her again something feral blazed inside him. Holding her stare, he slowly raised the fingers that were still wet with her pleasure to his lips and licked her residual cream from each of his fingertips.

Kylie's breath seemed to stutter in her chest, and he felt as if her heart started beating double time. He felt her body grow languorous and moist just watching his tongue as it moved between the spaces of his spread hand. When his tongue slipped out for another lick, Kylie bent down and captured his tongue in her mouth and sucked. She had to taste herself on his tongue and know that she was delicious. Impatient now, she started to rub and rock herself against his erection trying to communicate her eagerness.

"Are you trying to tell me something, Kylie?" Austin asked. "Are you trying to let your underperforming thoroughbred know what you want?"

"Yes, yes," Kylie panted increasing the rhythm. Her pace indicated that if he couldn't do what she needed him to do, she would do it herself.

Austin refused to take the hint. He didn't move. He just held her steady as she ground on him, her movements getting more frantic and desperate. "Tell me then, Kylie.

Tell me what you want and I will give it to you. What do you want, Ms. Derringer?" He buried his face into her neck.

Kylie didn't hesitate or pretend to be coy. "I want you to fuck me now, this instant — hard!"

Without saying another word, Austin lifted her off his lap, positioned her, and dropped her down onto the full length of his cock. Kylie screamed and started convulsing immediately. Her small body shook with her pleasure creating a ricochet reaction in Austin. He slammed into her one, two, countless times, all out, full in, unbridled and unrestrained, and felt as if explosions were going off in his brain. His world narrowed to this moment, this woman, and the pleasure she brought him. For the second time that night, he poured himself into her giving her everything. When he was finished, the world went black. He moved them to the bed and fell into the unconscious sleep of the deeply satisfied.

When he woke up, Kylie was gone. There was no trace of her. In direct contrast to how good his body felt, his mood instantly turned black. He woke up with a craving that only his employee could satisfy. It annoyed him that he couldn't turn around in the bed, pull her close, and bury his head between her legs — eat her pussy as his first meal of the day. Cheerios it was, he guessed, but he was bitter about it. He showered and dressed meticulously. He put on his business suit with slow, careful movements, which punctuated just how angry he really was. He wasn't a male stripper, a navy seaman on twenty-four-hour leave, or some drunken biker she'd picked up at a bar for a one-night stand. He was Austin fucking DeAngelis: entrepreneur, businessman, and multi-millionaire.

No woman could just fuck him and leave.

Chapter Six

Austin walked into work and headed straight for his office without looking Kylie's way. He turned his computer on and attempted to concentrate but the sight of his employee sitting at her desk seemingly unaffected by the passion they'd shared made him furious. He was at work and he shouldn't make a scene, but he was so angry that he couldn't think of one reason why he should fucking care. He was the boss. He could do whatever the hell he wanted.

"Ms. Derringer. Please come to my office." He didn't bother to get up from his desk but let his voice carry throughout the office, loud enough, that all heads, including Kylie's, jerked up at the command in his tone. Had he yelled when he called her? Who gave a fuck.

"Yes, sir. What can I do for you?" Kylie replied loudly. She was the spirit of politeness for the mere reason that she must have felt the eyes of a million programmers at her back.

Austin could have cared less about keeping up appearances. He flicked a switch and the see-through glass windows of his office went dark.

"What the hell are you doing?" she said in an angry whisper, closing the door behind her with a click. "Why don't you just make a company announcement that we slept together? It would be subtler than what you're doing now."

Without a word, Austin came around his desk, freeing himself from his pants and expertly donning protection as he walked. He reached her, picked her up, tore her panties off, and put her legs around his waist. With his fingers, he roughly probed her to gauge her readiness. Wet. Yes! Mindless, he positioned her, jerking up and into her without another word. His dick only got halfway to its destination before her body resisted.

"Ahh!!" she cried out, her head falling back, her mouth open.

"Lord, what have I done?" Austin swore. "I'm so sorry. God, what was I thinking." He began to withdraw.

Kylie locked her knees together to hold him in place. "It hurts," she muttered. "It really hurts."

Austin cursed and tried to withdraw. Again, Kylie wouldn't let him break free.

She looked down at her partially impaled body and licked her fingers and rubbed the moistness on that part of

Austin's anatomy that hadn't found its way all the way in. "That should help," she said breathlessly. "Because that hurt just now, but I liked it."

Austin swore as reason and caution again took a back seat to his own ravenous need. "Tell me when to stop and I will stop. Tell me... Tell me... Tell me," he repeated as all other thoughts left his brain.

Kylie placed her hands on his shoulder for leverage and then slammed herself down onto his dick, forcing him all the way in. The sensation was so satisfying that she did it again and again until her body was a slick passage for all of Austin's might and heat. He held still through her ministrations almost like he was punishing himself for taking her before she was completely ready. Kylie didn't mind; she used his body as payment, as compensation for all he felt he owed her. He didn't owe her anything, but Kylie liked the power it gave her to have Austin repentant and playing the role of submissive. It made her feel powerful, like the predator instead of the prey. She used him to pleasure herself like she wanted, until the pleasure crested and she buried her mouth into Austin's neck to muffle her scream. She was only barely aware of Austin bucking against her with short, violent thrusts, which lasted mere moments until all was quiet and still.

She climbed down off her boss, and when her feet hit the ground, she wobbled for just a second before she straightened. Damn. Damn. Damn! She hadn't meant to do that — fuck her boss, and in the office of all places. What the hell had she been thinking? Having the best sex in her life was no reason for her to kiss her professional reputation goodbye. She questioned her motives for wearing a skirt to work. She never wore dresses. Was she trying to make it easier for him? Had she secretly wanted just this outcome when she snuck out of his bed in the middle of the night? Kylie shook her head. She didn't understand herself.

"Can you turn that thing back on? It's been dark in here too long already." Kylie pulled down her skirt, sat in the chair across from the desk and placed her hands in her lap. She watched without comment as Austin pulled his zipper back up, straightened his tie, smoothed his hands through his hair, and sat down at his desk. He pushed a button and the privacy glass windows cleared.

"What do you have to say for yourself?" he asked. His voice was calm and without inflection.

He looked so relaxed, so unperturbed and elegant that Kylie was instantly irritated. She didn't need to look in the mirror to know what she must look like. She felt like a tumbled harlot and it probably showed. Sweat from her exertion was coaxing her hair into soft waves. She felt flushed and hot. Her skin prickled. Every inch of her body was in fight or flight mode. She was a mess. Austin was not. His dark skin revealed no evidence of his passion. His sleek silver hair didn't have a tress out of place. Only his eyes, which glittered with aqua fire, showed any evidence of emotion.

"I asked you a question." The words were clipped. Curt.

"I don't know what you mean, Mr. DeAngelis. Have I done something wrong?" After her shameless conduct just moments ago, she was the epitome of cool employee-employer professionalism.

Austin's eyes narrowed and he leaned back negligently in his leather executive's chair. The opulent chair's faint creak was the only sound in the room for long moments.

"Do you make a habit of having sex on the run?"

Kylie leaned forward abruptly. "Excuse me?"

"Did I stutter? I'm quite sure that you heard me." His voice was dark with some emotion.

"I wasn't aware that I was on the clock and required by my employer to put in a full eight hours." She was insolence itself, but he deserved it for being territorial.

"If you were on the clock, Kylie, I would have paid you for a job well done and sent you home in the company car. I'm asking why you left without a word."

"Did I hurt your feelings? Are you used to doing the leaving instead of being left? I don't have to explain myself to you, Austin. I had an awesome time. You, sir, are an amazing lay. But that's it. We agreed. Was there anything business-related you wanted to talk to me about?" She was conscious of the fact that no one was in Austin's office this long without reason. She smoothed her skirt before unfolding from the chair and tried to ignore the fact that Austin's eye followed every movement of her body as she stood up.

"Yes, that's all. But, from a purely business standpoint, I'm going to need you to work late tonight."

"Why?" she argued. "I have all the projects assigned to me handled. There's no need for that."

"If I feel there is a need, then there is. I'm the owner of this company; I'll decide what's necessary and what's not. Is that clear?" There was something forbidding and dark in his tone.

"...Crystal *clear*," Kylie said through clenched teeth. "May I go?" she asked with exaggerated politeness.

Austin waved his hand in the direction of the door. The gesture wasn't even complete before Kylie sailed out.

Austin watched her as she stomped back to her desk, an action that brought every man's head up. A woman in a skirt and combats boots shouldn't have been arousing but Kylie in any attire that showed her magnificent legs was worth watching.

Austin rested his head in his hands. What was he going to do with her, he wondered? This unreasonable craving had to stop. He hadn't meant for things to go this far. A taste, a touch, was all he wanted. He'd gotten more than he asked for. Kylie was... a wildcat. She was little and ferocious. She was a fantastic bed partner. She was unafraid, spontaneous, energetic, and sensual. He'd never met a woman who satisfied his need for violence and tenderness simultaneously. One day he would fuck her slow. He would take his time. He wouldn't come fast and hard like a callow youth but make the moment last until her muscles ached from his exertion. He would make her scream and beg and then teach her manners and respect.

Just thinking about the ways he would make her obey made his cock tent his trousers. Shit! He wanted her again. Austin glanced at his executive bathroom and wondered if he should call her back, sit her on the toilet seat, and stand over her with his pants down. He wanted to fill her saucy mouth with something other than words. He looked out his office door, considering putting his thoughts into action. It took him some time before reason could prevail. His brain cooled, his reason returned, but his cock still didn't get the message. Austin swore furiously and then abruptly stood up toppling his chair with the movement. He looked at Kylie through the glass windows one more time before he stalked to the bathroom and slammed the door behind him. His hard cock was already in his hand.

Chapter Seven

"Good afternoon, Mother." Austin embraced her. Because he was still angry, and edgy, from his pseudo-argument with Kylie earlier, he wasn't above making one woman pay for the transgressions of another. Feeling slightly vindictive, he wrapped both arms around his mother's slender frame, giving her an embrace just shy of a bear hug. As anticipated, she stiffened. To prolong the agony she felt from physical contact, Austin perversely lingered over the embrace, going so far as to rest his silver head atop her sleek black mane. He squeezed her tightly to his chest for good measure, and then released her.

She glared at him with pursed lips and her green eyes narrowed in displeasure. "I wish you wouldn't do that," she told him, her mouth pinched.

"Do what?" Austin asked. He was the picture of innocence and guile.

"You know *what*," she said shuddering as if to shake off his touch.

"I really don't," Austin went on without remorse. He gave his mother hugs now for all the times when he was young and yearned for them but had to do without. He knew it was petty, but he enjoyed rattling her.

They stared at each other with him smiling and her face blank, emotionless. He broke the stalemate when he approached her and fondly pecked her on the cheek. "You look beautiful as always, Mother. Is that Chanel? The silhouette on you is perfection!"

She turned away from him in a huff and went over to the desk where she wet a hand sanitizer on a tissue and scrubbed off the feel of his lips from her skin. The pinch Austin felt at her actions was slight these days, but he felt it nonetheless.

"Can I ask why you're here?" Her tone was stern, but she protectively wrapped her arms around her waist.

"I take it you're not delighted to see me?" Austin asked, plopping himself down on the luxurious sofa in his childhood home located in the Bridle Path section of Toronto.

"You're my son," she said as an answer.

"You sure?" Austin teased. "If I'm adopted you can tell me, you know."

78

His mother stared at him with concentration he found disconcerting. "No, you're mine. Look at you. That beauty certainly doesn't come from your father."

Austin's lips curled in an approximation of a smile. "Yes, I inherited my mother's good looks but nothing else."

"Yes, nothing else," she agreed, gathering her long hair in her hands and sweeping it behind one shoulder. They stayed that way in near silence before his father strolled in.

"Austin." His name was spoken like a command.

"Father," Austin responded. Unlike the show he made of interacting with his mother, Austin didn't even pretend to have a relationship with his father. His father didn't care. He gave his son the barest glance before his attention went to his wife. He lived with her, saw her every day, but every time Destin DeAngelis encountered his wife, it was like he was seeing her for the first time. She, of course, ignored him. So, like his son, he forced a reaction from her.

"Brinkley. Come here, please." It wasn't a request.

She went immediately of course, but after years of watching her, studying her every nuance and expression, Austin knew from years of analysis that the light unhesitating steps she took towards her husband whispered of a stilettoed trek towards the guillotine.

"What can I do for you, darling?" A hand loaded with heavy diamond jewelry slid around his waist. With the slightest hint of pressure, she leaned her slim body into his bulky frame. She made it look effortless and easy but watching her, Austin knew how much the daily display of devotion cost her. Every movement she made was practiced. She was well trained.

His father didn't care. If he suspected she hated him, he was content with the *demonstration* of love if not that actual feeling. His need for control and comfort, adequately satisfied with his wife by his side, he turned his awareness to his son.

"What brings you here? If you tell me it's Diavolo's house on the shore, I'll throw you out."

Austin's practiced, light-hearted expression darkened. "Why can't you sell it to me? You don't want it. Why do I have to wait until you die to get what belongs to me? Granddad meant it to be mine. You stole it from me to be spiteful. That old house means nothing in the scope of your empire. Give it to me. It's mine."

"Technically it's mine, son. The mere fact that you want it so badly tells me to hold on to it. Maybe I will want something from you in the future. That house is my collateral. Stop coming by to discuss your grandfather with me. He was my father. We didn't like each other. Yes, he loved you, but that was bad taste on his part. Now, if there is nothing else, your mother and I would like some time alone."

Because she stood their idle, mute, without an ounce of support or even an opinion, Austin gave his mother a feral smile and said, "Enjoy each other. Good evening." He turned and left, barely repressing the desire to slam the door.

Diavolo DeAngelis was the only person bearing his last name that Austin had ever loved. Whatever warmth, tenderness, care, and consideration that existed in him, he'd learned from his grandfather. His grandmother had died years before he was born so Austin and Diavolo were often together. A hostile father and a careless mother meant there weren't a lot of people to protest if grandson and grandfather spent twenty-four hours a day trading stories, telling tales, laughing, eating, and just delighting in each other. From his grandfather he had learned to be a man of honor. From him, he had learned the ins and outs of business. He had learned to be shrewd but fair.

He learned to protect himself from the daily rejections of his parents and had slowly become self-sufficient. Every secret, sorrow, vice, or victory he'd shared with Diavolo; the old man who listened and never lectured. He'd directed him towards better choices and wiser decisions without judgment. It was Diavolo that had listened with patience and compassion when Delilah had wrecked his self-confidence and torn a hole in his self-esteem. As he stalked to his car, he remembered that time in his life with grim memory.

"Austin, I love you." Delilah had looked at him with dark eyes that were fathomless before resting her head on his chest.

"No, you don't. How could you?" He'd meant the question earnestly. Delilah was a college-boy's wet dream. All shiny, long, dark tresses, smooth, blemish-free skin, and a body that was honed by cheerleading, a dedication to a strictly organic diet, and a rigorous, but mostly unnecessary, exercise regime.

Even at eighteen, he was nothing to sneeze at. However, back then, he'd worn his prematurely greying hair lank and long and, on lazy days, caught up in an unfortunate ponytail. Like most privileged suburban white teens, he'd suffered from an obsession with hip-hop and urban culture so he had worn his clothes a size or two too big. He'd been tall even then, but he'd been whipcord lean with no bulk to balance out his wide shoulders. Women had been attracted to him even before he entered college, but he could always tell that they were drawn to him because of his looks and his bank account.

Delilah was different. She said she loved him for who he was. He certainly thought he loved her. He loved her as much as he knew how to love anybody. For that reason, he was careful and solicitous with her every need and emotion. He knew that his size was daunting to many women. He'd spent a lot of his teen years being taught the intricacies of sex by horny caterers and housekeepers, bored housewives, rebellious and rich diplomats' daughters and on occasion, well-meaning and highly helpful family friends. They'd used him for pleasure, and he'd used them to ease the loneliness that at times overwhelmed him. His emotions had never been a factor.

Watching his parents interact, he knew from experience that love could be used to hurt and wound. He couldn't afford to let anyone do that to him. That changed when Delilah came into his life. He spent hours talking to her and she listened. She didn't ask for anything from him which made him all too eager to give her everything. She didn't ask him about his family; she respected his need for privacy and never tried to change who or what he was. Whenever he looked at her, he wanted to devour her, but he'd never been with anyone who wanted him for more than his looks and what he could give. Delilah wanted to wait for intimacy. She was careful never to touch him in any way that would set him off, which made the physical agony he felt every time he was around her even more acute. He respected her. He liked the way she loved him, completely and without pressure. For this reason, he was willing to grant her every wish. If he was honest, being with her sexually had scared him. From numerous complaints and compliments, he knew he wasn't like other men. He was bigger, thicker, and longer. Young boys are naturally curious, and from his early years in the locker room, his developing body had earned him both awe and envy from his school friends. To him, it was a nuisance. Girls liked the idea of extra-large men, but they didn't like it so much in reality. That combined with the fact that his parents' relationship was built around pain and pleasure, his mother's pain and his father's pleasure, meant that he was leery of what he could do to women if he lost control of himself.

He didn't want to be like his father in any way. Through the years, gossip had filled his young ears with enough info regarding his father's tendencies to paint a clear picture. So as in everything he did, he planned the seduction and consummation of his love with Delilah systematically, carefully, and with dedicated planning.

"Can I touch it?"

"Yes, you can," he said through gritted teeth every time he and his girlfriend had found themselves alone.

Soft hands glided over the thick head of his cock; a solitary finger slipped over the eager opening that wept desperate and starved tears. When she was feeling bold, she would grasp him with both hands and sweep the long staff between small hands from root to tip. Soon she became good at touching him, unafraid and aggressive, but through it all, she remained adamant that she was still afraid to try sex for real. She said he was too large for her. It would hurt, she complained. It was too soon, she insisted.

He respected her wishes and tried other ways of convincing her. He'd lay her down and spread her like an eager offering on the bed. He'd expose her sweet pink pussy to his gaze, to his lips, and tongue, making her wail from the pleasure he gave. He would bury his face in her mound and breathe in the sweet intoxicating smell of her, growing drunk from her special kind of perfume. He would take her small, perfectly round breast between his hands and roll the large, dusky nipples between his fingertips. He'd suck the distended tips until they glistened from his saliva. She would climax again and again until she collapsed, satisfied, in her narrow dorm room bed.

But still, she wanted to wait. He cared about her enough that he would have waited forever if he had to. Forever ended up not being as long as it could have been.

With his mouth set in displeasure, Austin got in his car and shook off the memory. How incredibly stupid and gullible he'd been. His idiocy still rankled over a decade later. Women made men stupid but not him, not ever again; he'd learned his lesson and learned it the hard way. For that reason, he would keep his head where Kylie was concerned. He didn't think she was half as devious as Delilah had been, but she was beautiful. Generally, beautiful women couldn't be trusted. Things came too easily for them and it made them spoiled, entitled, and uncaring. It was a horrible generalization but he'd yet to meet a woman that had shown him otherwise.

Chapter Eight

"Good morning, Mr. DeAngelis."

"Good morning, Nathaniel," Austin greeted the head of building security as he swept through the hotel lobby.

"Morning, Mr. DeAngelis." Another part of the security team greeted him.

"Eddie," Austin replied while still on the move.

"Have a good day, sir," another voice said.

"Thanks, Tommy." Austin acknowledged with a slight dip of his head. And so it went as he walked the length of the lobby to get to the elevators. He made it his business to know everyone who worked for him. What that meant, however, was that on a daily basis, he said what felt like a million *good mornings* before he'd even had his first cup of coffee. He was almost at the elevators when he heard someone shouting his name — loudly.

"Austinnnnnnnn. Yo, Austin!"

After the prior formality between himself and his employees, the casual use of his first name stopped him in his tracks. Austin turned and watched slightly chagrined as a large black man dressed in biker shorts, spiked bicycle shoes, sunglasses, a riding helmet, and a mail carrier bag slung across his body approached him with a wide grin. The man slapped him across his back with a whack and shook his hand.

"Austin, what's up man?"

"Ah... I'm doing just fine, thanks," Austin answered as he studied the man and tried to recall, without success, which of his acquaintances were in the message delivery business. He came up blank. "I'm sorry, have we met?" he asked finally, even as he subtly held a hand up to the security officers who looked ready to take the man down if asked.

The man pounded him on his back again, momentarily knocking Austin off balance. "It's me, man. Don't you recognize me?" And with that, he lifted black sunglasses from his eyes, whipped off his helmet, and stared at Austin expectantly.

"Kinky?" Austin guessed, even though he looked older and was minus his trademark dreadlocks and goatee.

"Who'd you expect? Yes, it's me." He gave Austin a smile and a wink.

Austin smiled back at the man, despite himself. They weren't old friends as Kincaid Murphy's presumption implied, but he remembered him fondly. "Kinky" had saved his life — literally. When he was seventeen and feeling rebellious towards his parents and the restraints they put on him, he'd fancied himself a thug prince, a hellion. He thought he was tough and invincible.

Following some friends from his private school, they'd ventured into a rough neighborhood in the West End of town to score some weed. A dealer had taken one look at them piled inside the Mercedes S class and took them for the mark they were. They were dragged out of the vehicle, robbed, and chased out of the neighborhood. Austin hadn't run. He'd resisted when they decided that the car should stay behind. They were in the process of beating the living daylights out of him when Kinky came on the scene. He'd pulled the other boys off him and gave him bus fare with a warning not to come into the neighborhood again.

"Thanks, man. What's your name?" Austin had asked the large black teen, his right eye already swelling shut.

It was an impertinent and somewhat perilous question considering his whereabouts, but Kincaid had smiled, shook his head in wonder, and answered anyway. "I'm Kincaid Murphy. Kinky to my friends."

Austin hadn't seen Kinky in years. After their initial meeting, Austin had looked up Kinky online and they'd kept in touch that way, but they'd lost touch. Later, when he was just starting out in the business world, he'd run into him delivering packages for FedEx, saw him selling tourist maps outside corporate buildings, and saw him delivering food to high rises among other entrepreneurial pursuits. They'd spoken at length every time. He liked Kinky. Always had.

"Is everything okay, sir? Is this man bothering you?" Tommy interrupted his musing by placing a restraining hand on Kinky's shoulder. He eyed the courier with a suspicion that he didn't bother to disguise.

Austin understood of course; it wasn't every day that a man who made millions and one that made minimum wage knew each other, much less had anything to talk about. "It's okay, Tommy. I know him."

"Yeah, step off, fool. I know him." Kinky shook off the guard's hand and made an elaborate production of brushing his touch from his shoulder. "Back up, brother. Don't you see I'm speaking to my man here?"

Austin gave Tommy a nod and the guard stepped back and away.

"Yeah, that's right. Begone! Give a man some space to breathe. Geez." Kinky's scowl was ferocious, but when he turned back to Austin, like magic, his smile was bright and cheerful again. Kinky spun around the elaborate foyer, eyeing the architecture. "This you, *dog*?"

"Yes, it's a new acquisition," Austin answered, amused.

"Well, well, look who's taking over the world."

Austin put his hands in his pockets and shrugged. "What about you? What happened to the food delivery gig?"

"Lost it or it lost me," Kinky answered. "But that's okay, 'cause I'm about my own money-making enterprise myself." He lifted the bag to show Austin the company logo. "Bad weather, rain, or sunshine – Kincaid Couriers will get it there on time!"

"Sounds promising, but you know my other offers still stand. If you want a job with one of my companies, it's yours. I respect your drive."

"Nah, I ain't a suit and tie guy. I'm doing okay on my own. Appreciate the business advice in the past though. Your input helped birth this new moneymaker. That said, if I ever need a stiff corporate 9 to 5, you're my man!" He threw his hand over Austin's shoulder and walked him to the elevator. "We should do dinner one night. I'll drop in, you can bring me to one of those fancy restaurants that gets nervous when a brother not in Brooks Brothers walks in, and we can catch up. What you say?"

"I'd like that, Kinky," Austin answered, meaning it. It was rare in his life that he had conversations that were genuine or real. When you had as much money as he had, inevitably you were surrounded by sycophants and yes men. Kinky didn't give a damn about his social stature or his business influence. To prove his point, Kinky thrust an assortment of envelopes into his hand. Austin looked down at the mail in confusion.

"I'm gonna hold you to that dinner, man. Watch out for me; you never know when this *Hungry Man* will come and collect. In the meantime, this little chat of ours got me running late. You on the top floor, right? That's for you and your staff. Deliver it for me. I gotta go." With one last companionable slap on the back, Kinky turned on his heels and strode off.

Austin looked helplessly down at the mail in his hand and started laughing. He stepped into the elevator and was still chuckling to himself when the doors opened onto the floor of his office. He dropped the envelopes off at the front desk. "See that those get to the right department, please." He was grateful that his administrative staff was so well-trained that no one thought to ask how he had gotten ahold of the mail in the first place.

Austin worked diligently throughout the day. He was focused. Making progress on the launch of his new product, Appian, held his full attention. The product's success in the marketplace was too important for him to have anything less than laser focus. He called in Brixton and consulted with the programming and development team. He identified potential problems. He was available for questions and open communication. He hadn't made himself this available on a project in years. He also usually left the design and development to his highly capable team, but Appian was different.

This project was his brainchild, his baby. If everything worked as he'd planned, it would be the first project he'd seen through from R & D to completion. He was a rich man already. He didn't need more money, but this project would make him wealthier than his father *and* his grandfather. It would make the DeAngelis name not just a legacy from an old and distinguished family, but something he'd built by himself for himself. He was under no one's shadow. His father could care less. The pressure Austin put on himself to achieve was self-induced. He was self-motivated. He wanted everything he touched to turn to gold — literally.

He reminded himself constantly throughout the day how important this project was to his future, to reaching and bypassing his personal goals. He did it to remind himself not to look in the direction of Kylie Derringer's cubicle. He did it so he wouldn't wonder if she'd looked up even once to watch him. She hadn't of course, not once. She was focused, resolute, and committed to her job. When she came into work every morning, her concentration was complete. He felt like an idiot for sneaking looks at her throughout the day, but he couldn't help it. He craved her.

To avoid being so fucking obvious, he grabbed the back of his neck and approximated a stretch that allowed him to turn his head yet again in the direction of Kylie's cubicle. He was pathetic! He felt like a high school girl. All that was left was for him to get his first period and grow boobs.

He didn't fool himself into thinking this sudden obsession was anything but physical. For a man who had to practice restraint in his dealings with women, Kylie's ability to handle him sexually was enough to have him salivating. He could go deep in her. He could go hard with her. He could let himself go for once in his life without the fear of causing discomfort or worse. He felt liberated from the need to hold back. That his emancipation came from a girl so tiny and petite was enough to blow his mind.

That she liked what he liked and saw his big dick as a challenge made him feel like this deal was nothing in comparison to the windfall waiting for him just outside his office door. Except, she wasn't waiting. At a glance, he saw that Kylie's cubicle was empty. Her purse was gone, and the little light she kept on during her workday was off. She'd up and left, just like that. Austin began absentmindedly grinding his teeth and a vein started to pulse in his forehead. Abruptly, the room of ten grew quiet and more than one person looked at him with concern. It was Brixton that spoke.

"Is everything okay, Austin?" Brixton looked at him with real concern.

Austin fought to pull himself together. "I'm fine. Can we table this discussion for another day? I have something urgent to take care of." *Urgent? Really?* He heard himself say it and would have slapped himself if he could. What was more urgent than his company and making shit loads of money? Sex never caused him to lose his focus before, but hell; there was a first time for everything. Austin grabbed his things and headed for the door.

The small and slightly shabby building had definitely seen better years. Concrete planters filled with wildflowers bordered the wide sidewalks, giving the area a quaint feeling. He inhaled the smell of spicy Jamaican food wafting through the windows of the restaurant at the corner which was in direct competition with the smells of marinara sauce and cheese from the Mom and Pop Italian pizzeria on the corner. His ears were attuned to the sound of someone's too loud car speakers blasting some mumble rap. Looking around, there were a lot more people loitering on the streets than he was used to seeing in his part of town, but they did so to mingle with friends and family members. The neighborhood vibe was hip, multicultural, and working class. It wasn't somewhere he would have chosen to live himself, but he'd never had to live on a fixed income.

In the Me-Too era, it was a bad idea to show up at Kylie's apartment unannounced. He acknowledged that his actions probably made him an awful person but still he strode up the stairs, taking them two at a time. He wondered as he neared her door what kind of reception he would get when she opened it and saw him. What if she had a man inside? What would he say? All these thoughts should have made him hesitate, but he didn't.

The sound of his knuckles on the wood door sounded loud. Nothing. When light taps didn't work, he pounded the door with his fist instead. Still nothing. He was moments away from kicking the door when it was wrenched open. Looking ferocious, Kylie Derringer stood on the threshold of her apartment. She was scowling.

"What the hell! Are you the goddamn police?" she yelled. "The fucking FBI better be behind you, Mr. DeAngelis. Better yet, I better be on the verge of getting arrested for stealing company property."

Austin blinked. No smile. No welcome. Not the reception he was hoping for. He didn't know he was hoping that she would grab him by his tie, give him a grin, a big kiss, and drag him into her apartment until it didn't happen. What was he thinking? This was Kylie. If she wasn't snarling, she was snapping on the best of days. He had just banged on her door like she was his dealer and he was a crackhead needing a fix.

But he did need a fix. Dressed in a skintight, one-piece, buttoned-up short's onesie, Kylie made him want to come by just looking at her. Her breasts were large and perfectly outlined. Cotton, which under normal circumstances was never sexy, defied expectation by hugging her curves and emphasizing the smallness of her waist, the firmness of her naked thigh, and outlining the beautiful V where her thigh met her pubic area. He wanted to drop to his knees in the hallway and eat her out. And eat her he would, wasn't that the reason he had come after all? Recalling his mission, Austin spoke. "May I come in?" he asked quietly, leaning his weight against the doorjamb.

"I'm off the clock, Mr. DeAngelis."

"But this isn't about work, sweetheart." Austin looked into her eyes. "This is about that other thing that we have going."

Instead of answering, she stared at him silently. "How did you find out where I live?"

"I misappropriated some HR files. I'm sorry but I was desperate."

"I hope you know, with one call this conversation we're having could make me very rich. This is borderline sexual harassment and stalking all wrapped in one."

"Tell me about it." Austin didn't contradict her. "I'm aware of the risks, but I don't care. Just the thought that you'll allow me inside you again is worth the risk."

Kylie inhaled loudly at his bluntness. She stood blocking the way into her home before stepping aside to let him in.

The apartment's interior wasn't what he expected. Pink and girly was out of the question, but he hadn't anticipated the almost industrial decor of Kylie's home. It was all metal, wood, and chrome. She used greenery to add warmth to what otherwise would have been a somewhat cold design aesthetic. It suited her.

"Nice place."

"Thanks. Can we skip the small talk?"

Austin blinked, surprised again. "Ah yeah, sure."

"Do you want a drink?" Her face was expressionless.

"No," he answered, wondering when he'd lost control of the situation.

"In that case," Kylie said releasing her hair from the topknot, "let's get started."

Kylie walked over to the bed that was against the wall of her studio apartment and began to remove her clothes. Austin froze. *That's right, Mr. DeAngelis* she thought to herself. No cajoling necessary. No discussion. She loved shocking him, and if his thunderstruck expression was an indication, she had caught him off guard...again. He

98

recovered quickly. He stepped further into the room, closed the door, and stalked towards her, each of his steps light and predatory. Helplessly fascinated by him, she couldn't help thinking he had a lot of nerve showing up at her apartment unannounced and uninvited. With that, she didn't fool herself into thinking that if he wanted he couldn't have been with anyone else, anywhere he chose. Part of her, a small part, wanted to be angry with him but another part of her was flattered. Maybe this wasn't just about scratching an itch. Maybe it was something more. *I must have lost my mind! I don't want him to fall for me... Do I?* The thought unsettled her. Forcing herself to focus, she idly stripped, making sure to linger, knowing he was watching. Wanting him to. Kicking away the garment, she sprawled on the bed.

"Don't just stand there, Mr. DeAngelis." She tapped a fingertip against her clit. "I want your tongue right here."

Austin was ravenous. Her words had inflamed him and her absence of shyness made him crazed. He'd never met a woman like her. The thought that after he put his tongue on her, he would shove his cock into her to the hilt made his breathing hitch. Before he knew what he was doing, Austin found his face between Kylie's thighs. He licked and sucked with abandon, tonguing her until she started panting.

"Do you like that, Kylie?" he asked, wanting to hear the raspy sound of her voice.

"Yes!" she said, threading her hands through his hair and pulling.

Austin's mouth was all over her. It astounded him all over again how small and petite she was. If he opened his mouth wide enough he could completely put her entire pubic area in his mouth. He tried it for fun. That it seemed possible made his balls draw up in excitement. He parted her lips with his tongue and started aggressively licking her clit. Kylie's reaction was explosive. She grabbed his head and ground her pussy against his mouth. She did this until her rhythm splintered. She cried out in ecstasy and collapsed on the bed in a heap.

"No wonder you're so popular with the ladies, Mr. DeAngelis. Your oral skills are off the charts. Most men need to be taught or given some instruction, but not you. You're a master." It was the closest she'd come to giving him a compliment.

Austin's mouth twisted. "Well, I had to be good at that, didn't I? If I was going to convince the women in my life to take on this monster," he said, grabbing himself through his pants, "I had to give them some incentive."

Naked, Kylie rose from the bed in a fluid motion and knelt in front of him. "You know what I think, Mr.

DeAngelis? I think that the women in your past were underachievers. You have an amazing cock and, as far as I'm concerned, it's a perfect size." To prove her point, she started unbuttoning his pants. She slipped her hands inside the slit of his boxers and he spilled into her hand.

Austin's head fell back at the sight of his dick in her small grasp. He appeared immense under normal circumstances, but in Kylie's small grip, he was huge. She wasn't intimidated. She gripped him with confidence and used both hands to stroke the length of him. She knew the perfect rhythm to make every hair on Austin's body stand on edge. When she put her pretty pink lips over the crown of his penis, he nearly came then and there. He knew Kylie would give him hell if he didn't rein himself in. She couldn't begin to understand what the sight of her soft lips moving up and down his shaft did to him. He wanted to thrust deep into her throat, pumping his length into her until all of him disappeared. That was impossible, but he wanted it more than he'd ever wanted anything in his life.

He was being greedy; excessive. It was a gift that Kylie could take all of him inside her body. Now, he wanted to fill every one of her holes? Yes! Yes, he wanted it. Because this woman made him greedy, he pumped himself deeper into her mouth. She swallowed the extra inch of him with ease. She slid up and down his length with an expertise that made him want to scream. He had never made a sound louder than a groan in his life. Having her suck his cock felt that good. She ran her tongue up the underside of his shaft and the sensation was so good that once she covered the head of his cock again with her mouth, he instinctively pushed himself further down her throat.

Kylie stopped abruptly and looked up at him with glistening lips. "Is this a test?" she asked, still stroking him with both hands.

His eyes rolled back, and his hips jerked with every downward swoop of her hands. He was almost beyond coherence. He wanted her to take in all of him so bad. "No, I'm sorry. I didn't mean to take advantage," he explained. His voice was strained. "What you're doing is fantastic. You make me forget all my hard-earned restraint. Continue, please?" Austin heard the plea and the near desperation in his voice but couldn't bring himself to care. If Kylie would give him more of what she was offering, then begging didn't have to be a bad thing.

"You're big," she said matter-a-factly.

"God, I know," Austin panted. "Just take as much of me as you can."

Kylie laughed, and Austin thought his head would explode when her breath washed over the head of his penis. He grunted loudly almost in near pain when Kylie took his penis in her mouth again and covered the head with her lips. From there, she went down the shaft, then went further and then further still. She pushed past her gag reflex to take more of him in, until with another slide, she had him almost down her throat to the hilt.

"Holy fuck!" Austin shouted.

She slid back up and repeated the process all over again until Austin's whole body started to hum. Watching her was one of the most erotic things Austin had ever seen. It was too much. It was too good. He was about to lose his mind. This little slip of a girl was destroying him without even trying. He wanted to have a fraction of the effect on her that she had on him. He abruptly pulled himself from her mouth. He picked her up, even as she gasped a protest, and threw her on the bed.

"Enough!" he growled.

"I wasn't finished." She licked her lips.

"Don't worry, baby." he said loving the way she looked all flushed and pink in the bed. "I will finish you. Tell me how you want it."

"You know how I want it," she said looking at him through lowered lashes.

Austin didn't pretend to misunderstand. "Yes, I do." With that, he crawled onto the bed and slipped his fingers inside her to gauge her readiness. "God, you're soaking wet."

He could feel the mindlessness that always came over him when he was in bed with Kylie.

"I was soaking wet from the minute I opened the door," she confessed.

He needed no further encouragement. Taking himself in hand, he positioned himself at her opening and thrust deep.

Kylie's back bent off the bed and she threw back her head in ecstasy. "Yes!" she screamed.

Austin thrust again, burying himself balls-deep. He couldn't describe the feeling. It was too profound for words. All he knew was that he wanted this woman. He wanted to be just like he was with her forever. She wouldn't welcome such an arrangement, but he would make her addicted to his touch so saying no was not an option. Austin set about pleasuring Kylie Derringer so that, for the rest of her life, she would crave no man's touch but his.

Austin was conspiring even as his silver head rested peacefully on Kylie's naked stomach. He felt soothed and agitated all at once as she aimlessly combed her fingers through his hair. She liked his hair, he thought. She touched it every chance she got. Many women had found the color peculiar, strange or weird, but this woman seemed to appreciate that his hair made him unique.

"What do your parents do for a living?" he asked, trying to sound casual.

He felt her stiffen. It was the first personal question he'd ever asked. He was desperate to know more about her. Where did she come from? What drove her? What made her laugh...or cry? He already knew so much about her that she hadn't told him. He knew what he had learned from observing her. He knew she didn't like strong emotions. She worked hard to mask all of her feelings. The only place she let her inhibitions down was in bed. She was a consummate professional at work but dressed like a Goth male stripper. He knew she was free-spirited but disciplined. She was a walking contradiction. She hid a lot and didn't let people in. What would it take to get past all those self-imposed barriers? What was hiding beyond all the boundaries?

"Why don't you tell me about yours instead?" she said finally when the silence stretched too long.

"There's not much to tell that hasn't been in the papers or on the news. My father inherited his money, my mother married into money, I make money and we're all one big unhappy family. Your turn."

"Why do you want to know, Mr. DeAngelis? Our arrangement hardly requires that we exchange family lineage."

"I want to know because you interest me, Kylie. You're an enigma made up of all these delightful contradictions and

I want to know which part of your history is responsible for the delightful mix."

"That's a pretty way of saying that I'm strange." She laughed but only with the barest hint of humor. "I'm an only child. My father, who I barely know, was a soldier and was missing for most of my life. My mother is...*was* a hairdresser until she fell on hard times. I grew up here and have never been anywhere else of interest. The end."

"Hairdresser, you say? No wonder you have an appreciation for this mane of mine," he tried to lighten the mood.

"Oh yes," Kylie agreed, tightening her grip on his hair and drawing his head back so their eyes met. "I love your hair. It's my favorite part of you; makes me think of lightning, stardust, and glitter."

"I'd prefer if it made you think of steel, gunmetal, and titanium. Those are manlier. And if that's your favorite part of me, I have been lax in not making you fall in love with some other part of my anatomy."

"I like the other parts just fine." Her tension seemed to melt away. "You're a beautiful man. If I was a different type of woman, I would be half in love with you already."

"Only half?" Austin questioned. In his mind, he was already dissecting her statement, seeking points of vulnerability. Half in love would never do. He needed Kylie to want to breathe the air he breathed if just for the sake of seeing his chest move. He wanted her to see his face when she looked in the mirror. He wanted her to wake up with his name on her lips.

He'd never wanted anything half this bad before.

Chapter Nine

Kylie made her way to her mother's apartment building with a light step. The sun was still shining but the changing season announced itself with slightly colder temperatures. Fallen leaves were scattered on the concrete. Kylie kicked a few playfully and strode on. With her headphones on, she skipped through her Nirvana, The Sisters of Mercy and Siouxsie, and The Banshees playlist until she found her favorite old-school Bon Jovi track. She sang out loud and just because she could, she stopped in the middle of the sidewalk and sashayed her hips to the beat. She smiled self-consciously when a teen on his skateboard clapped. She gave him a smile, moved past him, and then abruptly stopped in her tracks a few steps further.

Wait a second. She was in a good mood — a really good mood. It was Thursday, she was visiting her mother and still, she had a smile on her lips. What was the reason? The answer made her frown. *Austin*. His visit, and the days that

109

followed where he found her in different parts of the building, secret places, and made her body hum and sing. His attention, and the anticipation of seeing him each day, made her days bright.

Fuck. Was she whipped? Hooked on the dick? The answer was yes. She hadn't seen it coming. Her steps slowed and she pondered what to do about this disturbing discovery. Austin was not the kind of man a woman made herself care about and she was not the type of woman who did the caring. She needed to do something. Cut him off? Just the thought alone was excruciating. She couldn't decide now. She'd get through this visit with her mother and then come up with a plan. She opened her mother's door with the key, expecting to find her in her usual robe and slippers. Instead, Lana was fully dressed.

"Hey, Mom, are you going out? Did you forget it's our day together?" Kylie asked.

"No, I didn't forget, Kylie. I have somewhere to go. Will you come with me?" Her mother's face was grim, and her lips pinched.

"Of course, I will, Mom. Where to?"

"You'll see," Lana answered, offering no further explanation.

The doctor walked back into the room with a chart in his hand. Both Lana and

Kylie looked at him expectantly. Neither of them was prepared for what he was going to say next.

"When you came to us a few months ago your mammogram test gave us cause for concern. The fatigue, the loss of appetite, and the trouble breathing pointed to a serious health condition. The lump in your breasts needed to be looked at again for a conclusive diagnosis. Back then, we urged you to come in for a follow-up right away. Despite repeated attempts to contact you, you didn't contact us for the necessary follow up tests until recently." The doctor fluttered the paper in an imperceptible sign of frustration and said, "I am sorry to say that your test results aren't good. You have breast cancer and it has metastasized."

"Metastasized?" Kylie stared at the doctor. "What does that mean?" A sense of foreboding came over her as she waited to hear what he would say next.

He turned to her mother. "It means that you're very sick. We may have to remove the breasts, but it may already be too late for that. If so, we'll have to explore what else can be done to increase your chances. It means that the treatment I propose will be aggressive. The oral chemotherapy drugs prescribed that have worked for postmenopausal women such as yourself are historically not covered by insurance and are very expensive." His eyes softened in sympathy at her mother's look of fear. "I wish you had come back when I asked but we still have options. We still have a chance."

"A chance?" Lana asked, clutching the hospital gown to her chest, hands shaking. "Speak English, doctor! A chance for what?"

"...survival," the doctor and Kylie said simultaneously.

Kylie watched as the blood drained from her mother's face. Cold suddenly swept through her. She and her mother exchanged looks of disbelief. At the growing quiet, the doctor hastened to fill the yawning silence.

"You can fight this. With the right care and the right treatment, you can have a quality life," he said trying and failing to be reassuring. "In recent years the survival rate for breast cancer has increased tremendously. I have every confidence that the outcome will be positive. I'll go see how early we can get you started on a program. We don't have any time to lose."

He stood and left them together in the room. They both were too dazed to speak. Her mother broke the silence first.

"But my breast, Kylie; my wonderful breasts," Lana wailed as she cupped the mounds in her palms. They spilled over her small hands.

"You don't need them," Kylie said harshly, cutting off any form of discussion. She was afraid for her mother and the fear made her abrupt.

"I do need them," Lana insisted. Tears streamed down her face as she massaged her breasts. "I'm not that old. What kind of woman will I be without them?"

"A woman that's alive" Kylie's temper was now flaring. It occurred to her in a rush of horror that Lana might not agree to surgery if it was still needed or the grueling treatment that followed.

Her mother turned toward her, and Kylie strived for gentleness.

"They've made a lot of headway in reconstructive surgery," Kylie tried to persuade her. "We can buy you a new pair; bigger and firmer than the ones you have now. You'll have the breasts of a twenty-one-year-old. Wouldn't you like that? They'll be even better than mine."

Lana gave her daughter an incredulous look. "Really, Kylie," she said shaking her head. "Don't be ridiculous. As if anyone's breasts could be better than yours."

Frowning, Kylie looked down at her breasts covered in a white tank top layered with a black, knit, shredded sweater. She looked up at her mother in confusion.

Lana sighed in exasperation. "Christ, Kylie, sometimes your obliviousness amazes me." She bit her lips and turned away but not before Kylie spotted the tears spilling down her mother's cheeks.

Her irritation fled, replaced with fear. This was real. She could lose her mother. She reached out and grasped Lana's hands and didn't comment on how hard her mother returned the grip.

"I know you're scared, Mom, but I need you to take this seriously ..."

With new compassion in her voice, Kylie smoothed her mother's hair and spoke as gently as she knew how, "I know this is scary, Mom. But I need you to take this seriously. I need you. You're the only family I have. I can't bear the thought of losing you. We haven't always gotten along and a lot of that may be my fault, but I want us to have a future together. Please, I'm begging you. Take this seriously. Do it for me." As the last words left her mouth, from out of nowhere, emotion clogged Kylie's throat bringing her to tears.

"Kylie?" her mother said in astonishment. "Are those tears for me? Oh baby." She gathered her daughter up in her arms. "There's no need for this. Of course, I'll go through with the surgery if needed and any treatment the good doctors recommend. I don't want to die. But you heard the doctor, even with Ontario's health plan, I don't know how we'll pay for all this. I won't sacrifice my health for my vanity though, especially now that I know how much you need me." She spoke with a hint of astonished bewilderment.

"Of course I need you, silly woman," Kylie said in exasperation while wiping her tears with her sleeve. "You're my mother. All women need their mothers."

"Yes," Lana smiled. "Yes, they do."

"Don't worry about the money. I have a job. I'm permanent there now, and that change came with a hefty raise. We'll get you the best care that money can buy." It was a lie, but Kylie vowed to make it the truth.

"I'm scared, Kylie," her mother admitted.

Kylie hugged her mother hard. "Yeah, I know. I'm scared too."

Austin's butt hadn't even hit the chair that morning before Kylie breezed in.

"I'll take the job!" she announced.

He looked up from his desk. "I beg your pardon?"

She gave him a chance to sit and then moved further into the room. She stood directly in front of him. "You offered me a permanent position with benefits and a pay increase a while ago. If it's not too late, I'd like to accept."

Austin dropped the pen in his hand onto a stack of papers and gave her his full attention. Leaning back in his chair, he linked his fingers together behind his head and studied her face. "If I remember correctly, you weren't interested when I offered you the job. What's changed?"

"Nothing's changed. You offered me a job. It was a good offer, and I'd like to accept."

"We've moved forward on the project. We're interviewing a documentation specialist. It's too..." He didn't get to finish his sentence because Kylie was already speaking.

"Austin." Her already throaty voice deepened. "Please," she begged.

Austin sat up straight in his chair, his eyes alert. "Sure, Kylie," he said, studying her intently. "You were the first choice anyway."

"Excellent. Can I go talk to HR and get the paperwork started?" Her tone was almost shrill.

"Sure, you can but..."

"Okay, I'm going to speak with Beatrice right now then," she cut him off. "Thanks again." Kylie was halfway to the door before a hand clamped down on her arm.

"Not so fast."

She looked down at his fingers entwined around the delicate bones of her wrist and then back up at him. "Was there something else?"

"Kylie, what's wrong?" Austin asked softly. He rubbed his thumb against her skin.

"Nothing," she said abruptly, trying to twist her hand free. She didn't want to discuss her mother's health with anyone. Kylie was afraid she'd lose the grip on her emotions. That was out of the question.

Austin didn't let go. "Kylie, tell me what's wrong," he insisted.

Kylie looked to see if any of her coworkers would see her emotional breakdown. Wanting so much to talk to somebody, anybody, about her fears, she felt as if she might explode with the pent-up emotion she'd tried so hard to contain. She wanted to throw herself in Austin's arms and cry her eyes out. She was also desperate not to give in to her inclinations. As if sensing her struggles, Austin pressed the remote on his desk, darkening the windows of his office.

"What did you do that for?" Kylie protested. "What will people think?"

"They will think that I am having a private conversation in my office with one of my employees. The same type of conversations I have every day with any one of them. Now stop stalling. Tell me what's going on!"

Kylie twisted her mouth in wry amusement. Leave it to a man who was used to giving orders to demand confidence. The smile was fleeting. Her lips turned down almost instantly and then started to tremble.

"Ah, sweetheart." Austin released her wrist so he could tip her face up to his with his fingertips. "Whatever it is, it can't be that bad."

"It's my mother," Kyle said with a sob. "She's very sick."

"What's wrong with her?" Austin's hands were absently running through her hair.

"The doctor says she has cancer, and it's spread. I'm so scared. She's all I have." Kylie was trembling.

"It's okay, sweetheart," Austin reassured her. "Toronto has some really good hospitals and some of the best doctors in the country."

"I know." Kylie sucked in a breath, trying to contain the swell of emotion that was so foreign to her. "I'm not used to dealing with things I can't control."

"She'll be alright. What can I do? I know you just accepted the job, but do you need some time off? Let me help." The offer came with a tissue to wipe her eyes.

"No! No time off," Kylie pulled herself from his grip. "Time off is the last thing I need. I need to focus on something, and this project is as good as any other distraction."

"You'll tell me if there is anything I can do for you, right?" He was looking into her eyes with such intensity that Kylie couldn't look away. Something in his gaze made her want to trust him and to lean on him. The need to rely on someone was an alien sensation. She'd only relied on herself since she was a child.

In that moment, she felt close to him, as though what they had was more than sex, more than just *physical* intimacy. She wanted to reward him in some way for showing her such kindness. It was her experience that men rarely did anything without seeking payment, so she made a habit of never having to ask anyone for anything for that reason. But in this moment, in the relative seclusion of her boss's office, she felt for the first time in a long time, that someone cared.

"Thank you, Austin." She looked up at him from lowered lashes. She shifted closer to him when just moments ago all she'd wanted to do was get away. "I appreciate your wanting to help me. I can't thank you enough... Or can I?" Her hand drifted down in the direction of the impressive mound beneath the crotch of his trousers. Her hand fluttered delicately against the swell and then massaged it with more purpose. Her boss sucked in a harsh breath and then let it out with a hiss. She gave him a half-smile and began to unzip his fly.

His hand clamped down on hers. "Don't," he said, his gaze level, serious and resolute despite the passion smoldering beneath the surface. "Kindness is not a debt you need to repay, Kylie." At her look of confusion mixed with mild astonishment, he tapped the tip of her nose and gently pushed her away. "You needed a friend just now, and I was happy to be there for you. There's no charge for compassion. I care about what happens to you."

"I don't understand," Kylie frowned, truly mystified. It was her experience that men never turned down sex. No matter the reason. But Austin was telling her no. She felt a strange stirring in her chest. She wanted to massage the sensation away, but it only intensified. The feeling was warm. It was stronger than anything she had allowed herself to feel in a very long time. She backed up abruptly, almost stumbling over her feet in her haste. She didn't have time for anything beyond casual relationships with people of the opposite sex. She'd learned that relying on men only led to heartbreak. Austin — playboy, ladies' man, and rich, privileged jetsetter — was no different. The second she let herself forget that would lead to disaster.

"Okay, well let me know if you want a rain check," she said awkwardly, not meeting his gaze.

"Thanks, Ms. Derringer," he gave her a mocking grin. "I will keep that in mind."

Chapter Ten

...*Wear something pretty.* Kylie examined her closet, trying to fulfill Austin's request. Unfortunately, pretty didn't factor into the clothes she had hanging there. She had comfortable clothes and one or two things, that for her could be loosely considered conservative for job interviews and such, but pretty... Ah, no. Austin was shit out of luck. She stood in front of her closet in a scanty mesh panty and bra set that revealed all her best assets. She liked wearing risqué underwear under her somewhat combative clothes because it gave her the feeling of being naughty in a way that no one could see. The set made her feel sexy. She liked the way it was safely shielded from view but revealed everything without even a nod to modesty.

She'd like to have Austin see her in these and would want him to rip the mesh with his teeth, tear the scraps of fabric from her body, and bind her hands with the scraps of what remained. God, she was out of control where he was concerned. He was unraveling her discipline in the worst ways, but she liked the results. She tried to be prudent and impersonal with him, but he demanded everything and still wanted more. Kylie leaned her head against the cold wall and tried to get herself back under control.

"Pretty. Austin said to wear something pretty!" she said out loud, not knowing why she was torturing herself. It was just dinner. He was taking her out to cheer her up and get her mind off her mother. It wasn't a date really, but she wanted to look good. She contemplated running over to her mother's and dragging out something frothy from her collection, but decided against it. In the end, she decided to be herself and reached for the only option in the closet that came close.

Austin's world narrowed. Every inch of him stilled, grew taut, tight and agitated. He felt a strumming through his blood, a ringing in his ears, and lost the ability to hear anything except the clicking sound of Kylie's four-inch stilettos. *Wear something pretty,* he'd said! What the fuck! Was this Kylie's idea of pretty? Lord help him.

The dark, Mediterranean waiter assigned to his table and the short Hispanic busboy on his way to the kitchen both stopped dead in their tracks. Shoulder-to-shoulder, they stood beside Austin and openly stared. Kylie had blow-dried her hair straight and wore it tumbling wildly down her back with tendrils caressing the cups of overly-generous breasts. Austin's mouth went dry. The breasts that had factored so greatly in his dreams lately were encased in a leather crop top that bared her décolletage and her toned midriff. As if this wasn't enough, she paired the top with a pair of leather looking tights. Her legs looked as if they would never stop.

Lastly, because she was Kylie, around her neck, a silver nameplate necklace rested against the curve of her breasts in a spot that Austin had already decided he wanted to lick. No purse of course, but a single diamond link chain looped around her waist. This chain held the smallest mini-purse that couldn't possibly hold more than a tube of lipstick and a few bills. She walked up to him confidently. Rising on her tiptoes, she kissed him on the lips. Because she was closer to eye level with the heels, Austin reached out and dragged her back, savoring the feeling of her hips almost resting against his. Just looking at her made him start thinking of ways he could forgo dinner and go straight to bed. The patrons of the restaurant were looking at him. Austin realized he was making a fool of himself.

He elbowed both the busboy and the waiter in their sides to get their attention. He did it twice before they finally moved. When they were partially alone, he found his voice enough to say, "You look...ah...pretty."

Kylie gifted him with a sly grin. "I aim to please."

"Right over here," Austin indicated the table set for two. It was tucked away from prying eyes.

"Nice," Kylie commented as she took in the beautiful place setting.

Austin made sure there were fresh flowers on the table. They looked as if they'd just been picked. He told Kylie to wear something pretty, so for his pseudo-date, he'd also dressed carefully. He felt her studying his slate-grey suit jacket, his indigo and grey-colored scarf, and his dark-wash jeans, which were paired with an indigo tie.

"You're looking well-groomed and aggressively fashionable as usual Mr. DeAngelis," she said. "You almost make a girl feel underdressed."

"Why the formality, Kylie? After all the places I've kissed, sucked, licked, and nibbled on, surely, we can be on a first-name basis. Besides, I like you undressed. The less you're dressed, the more I enjoy looking at you. Wait! Is that a blush I see? Why Ms. Derringer, I'm shocked. Have I embarrassed you? How cute is that?" He was delighted.

"I'm not embarrassed, *Austin*." She said his name with force. "I'm just not used to talking about my exploits in a place where everyone can hear."

"...*Everyone*?" Austin made a production of looking over the high backs of the booth's chairs. Their nearest neighbor was more than a few feet away. He paid for privacy. "It's just me, baby. I want to talk about what we do together. It excites me. Tell me I'm not alone here."

Kylie looked into his eyes. "You're not alone. Not really. Unlike you though, I think talk is overrated. I'd rather show you what thoughts of you do to me. Shall we leave?" she offered.

Austin swallowed hard, his Adam's apple bobbing in a mostly dry throat. He wanted to leap from the chair and make his way to the closest exit as fast as his feet could go, but he was building something with Kylie here. Something he couldn't explain. All he knew for sure was that he wanted to get to know her better. "No, let's not leave. Not yet. I need you to be well fed so that you can provide optimal performance. If I give you the culinary fuel you need, you will perform for me won't you Kylie?"

"Oh, yes!" Her eyes came to rest seductively on his.

The waiter approaching their table broke the tension between them. "What can I get for you?"

Austin waved his hand in her direction. "Ladies first."

Kylie looked up at the waiter and smiled. "What do you have that will make a carnivore happy? No salads or any of that girly stuff. Tell me about your steaks, your surf and turf, or your restaurant's versions of a *Hungry Man Special*. I'm starved," she said laughing.

The waiter couldn't drag his eyes away from her enough to even recite the written specials printed on his menu pad. He was transfixed. It took him more than two beats before he stopped watching Kylie with a hunger far greater than the one she had described.

Clearing his throat audibly, he said, "For Miss, we can make anything you'd like. May I suggest something that might delight you?" His accent thickened. "I suggest the Filet Mignon in a peppercorn sauce served on a bed of fresh broccoli with a side of German- fried potatoes. We'd serve that with an exquisite red merlot. For dessert, oh Miss," he said, kissing his fingertips dramatically, "a chocolate mousse so deliciously prepared that it will make you forget your own name."

"Perfect!" Kylie grinned from ear-to-ear. "I'll take it. My *friend* here will have the same. He's ravenous."

The waiter looked at Austin slyly and said hesitantly, "Ah, so the gentleman is not your *sweetheart*, Miss?" The hopeful tone was hard to mistake.

"Back off, hombre." Austin's voice was deep with warning.

The waiter looked at him, bowed, and then, stepped back with his hands crossed over his heart. "As you wish, sir, but if the miss would like anything, anything at all..." he said pushing his luck. "Please ask for me personally. I'm Alexandre...at your service."

Austin's mouth twisted. "I think we have just about everything we need, how about that steak?"

Only after a reluctant and hopeful look thrown Kylie's way did the waiter finally take the hint and leave.

"...So much for his tip," Austin grumbled when the waiter was gone. "See, you make men crazy everywhere you go."

"I doubt that," Kylie said with humor. "If people turn to stare at me it's usually because they find my clothes fascinating... and not in a good way." She smiled down at her hands. "This is the most dressed up I've been in a while and still it isn't what most would consider proper five-star restaurant attire. I considered putting on a dress, but it just wasn't me."

Austin reached across the table and took her hand in his. He played with her fingers, with their black-cherry nail polish for a while, before his eyes met hers. "I love the way you look. I love the way you dress. I enjoy you as you are, Kylie. You're unconventional and the most interesting woman I have ever met. I like dresses like most men, but on you, I'll take tight leather any day."

Kylie's cheeks heated at the compliment.

"There it is again," Austin crowed in delight. "I've made you blush, not once, but twice. Who knew all it took to breach the defenses of the impenetrable Ms. Derringer was some sincere praise. I feel like I've just discovered the lost city of Atlantis!"

"Stop it, you troublemaker. Let's talk about something else."

"Like what?"

"Well, most first-outing conversations usually run along the lines of family and friends. Let's start there. You know what's going on with my mother. What's yours like? Does a powerful man like you have any real friends?"

Austin thought about her question and then said, "I'm an only child. My mother defies explanation. I'll take you to meet her because she must be seen to be believed. As for friends, I don't have many. Brixton you know. We've been friends since college. Then there are some acquaintances, but no one I'd have over for dinner."

"You have a very tight and exclusive circle, Mr. DeAngelis."

"Yeah, I do. What about you?"

"Only child, remember? At least I think I am. My father isn't exactly what you'd call the responsible type. I'm the only kid he's admitted to and that's because I'm a dead ringer. We're not close. Then there's my mother. She's a hairstylist as I've mentioned before. She lives in North York. I visit her as much as I can. I didn't grow up with a lot and everything I have, I've had to get on my own. A vastly different upbringing than yours I'll bet?"

"Yeah, except for the parents part. My folks and I aren't that close either. No friends?" He asked.

"I have girlfriends, but even the most dedicated friend starts to lose interest when you cancel one too many dinner dates so you can work. I've been a bit obsessive about my career for the last couple of years. I wanted to make a place for myself and I sacrificed things like close relationships to get there. Does that make me anti-social?" Kylie laughed self-consciously, probably thinking she'd revealed too much of her life.

Sensing her discomfort, Austin put his hand under her chin and lifted her face. "In case you haven't noticed, I'm auditioning for the new best friend role. I'd love to be your girlfriend," Austin said flipping long phantom tresses over his shoulder. When he got the required chuckle, he continued, "Seriously though, I think we could both do with a friend or two. Let's start now. Hi, I'm Austin, your new BFF."

"I don't know if a millionaire BFF is what I had in mind," she said with a smile.

"We make the best kind," he argued. "We won't ever ask you for money. We won't borrow your car or ask you to spend the night. Scratch the last one. I'm keeping that best friend privilege. I'd kill to see you in a face mask, curlers, and flannel pajamas."

"...Really?" Kylie's voice was filled with cynicism. "I'm positive the women you are used to only wear Agent Provocateur and La Perla."

"True." Austin didn't even try to deny it. "But flannel on you is as sexy as lingerie on anyone else."

Kylie's mouth twisted ruefully. "Damn, you're good," she admitted. "I respect that."

"Yes, I'm good," he agreed. "But what makes me better is how sincere I'm being. Now let's end this talk of lingerie and sleepovers or you'll find yourself spread out on the table as my main meal."

The waiter returned with their meals. Austin motioned to their plates. "Let's eat."

They ate in near silence, interrupted by brief periods of conversation. Getting details out of Kylie was like running up a steep hill. Thankfully, as dinner progressed, she let small details slip and relaxed with him as much as someone like Kylie could relax. As she ate, he found he liked watching her mouth move and enjoyed the way her lips formed around words. He liked the huskiness in her voice. Everything about her was a turn on.

By the time dessert came around and Kylie attacked her chocolate mousse, licking the spoon and moaning as the mousse touched her tongue; Austin's dick was already hard.

"Sorry to carry on like this," Kylie said slightly embarrassed as another moan slipped past her lips. "It's just that I've never tasted anything this good before."

Austin clenched his fist beneath the table and forced a smile. He had something delicious he wanted her to taste. If she enjoyed him even a fraction as much as she did her dessert, he would be a happy man. He tried tamping down any licentious thoughts with hopes of getting through the dinner. He wanted to get to know Kylie and that would never happen if they spent all their time fucking.

"Do you mind if we make a stop before I bring you home?" he asked near the end of their meal.

"Of course not," she agreed without hesitation.

The pseudo date had gone well and he was sure that he'd succeeded in taking her mind off her mother's health crisis. Earlier, she'd been consumed with worry. Dinner was the distraction she needed.

"Where are we going?" she asked when they were in the car.

"You'll see," he promised in a friendly tone. If she'd looked at his hands as they gripped the steering wheel, however, she'd have seen that his knuckles were white.

They pulled up in front of a home that could only be described as palatial. The three-story French-chateau designed home with its grey-washed brick, moss-covered façade that shielded twenty-plus perfectly symmetrical windows (she'd counted), was enough to make the blue-collar girl in Kylie stare with open-mouthed wonder. In a daze, she allowed Austin to drag her from the car and across the cobbled circled driveway. Unimpressed, he didn't even pause to take in the home's manicured lawn, mature trees, or the fountain that bubbled with what Kylie was sure must have been champagne. Instead, he briskly walked up to the front door, and to her astonishment, pushed it open without knocking and walked in.

"Austin, who is this may I ask?" Kylie looked to the entryway where an older woman stood centered below a fifteen-foot-high archway. Her face was pleasant and pretty but her polite tone held an edge and a bite.

"Kylie, this is my mother — Brinkley Beckett DeAngelis," Austin introduced them.

"It's nice to meet you," Kylie said, finally getting the words out after throwing Austin a look that said *what the fuck*! They each stood in a frozen tableau on the threshold of one of the most elegant houses Kylie had ever seen. She fought the urge to dip into a curtsy; the woman in front of her projected that much majesty. Instead, she extended her hand.

Austin's mother stared at her hands before grasping her fingertips and giving them an anemic shake. "I'm sure it is, dear," she said at last. "This is certainly a surprise. Austin doesn't bring anyone here to meet me."

"This is not a social call," he explained. "It's just that we talked about you earlier and I told Kylie that you had to be seen to be believed."

Kylie stared at Austin's mother's face. She did not betray any emotion. It was as if she was a masterpiece created by a brilliant painter, capturing beauty without a hint of the soul beneath.

She ushered them into a sitting room and gracefully sank onto a settee. As if they were alone together, Brinkley turned to her son. "I hope you're not planning on keeping this one, Austin. Her look is... how should I put it, unconventional to say the least." She stared at Kylie perched uncomfortably on the settee. "I see the reason for the attraction of course." His mother assessed Kylie as if she was

133

a piece of meat. "She's lithe, comely, and curvaceous. She's obviously talented in other respects, but Austin, those clothes. Surely the leather look outside of the nightclub isn't the trend these days."

Kylie visibly relaxed. She moved back onto the settee, the action making her feet nearly leave the ground despite her sky-high heels. Comfortably sprawled, she listened to the exchange. She knew she should be offended, and she was, but the statement was so like her own mother's that it brought a smile to her lips. It seemed that opposition to her attire crossed all socioeconomic lines.

"I amuse you, dear?" The previous frost in Brinkley's voice had deepened to an arctic chill.

"No," Kylie said trying without success to wipe the smile from her lips. "It's just that you remind me of my mother."

Brinkley drew herself up. "Indeed?"

"Yes, she doesn't like my clothes either," Kylie explained laughing.

Brinkley took a breath to say something, but Austin cut in. "I like your clothes, Kylie. I like them strewn across the floor. I like them tossed over a chair. I like them crumpled in a heap. I like everything about your clothes, when you wear them, and when you don't."

Both women frowned at him.

"Was that necessary?" Kylie asked, exasperated. "Your mother already has an instant dislike for me. Do you have to make it worse?"

Austin smiled widely. "God, I love that you're not easy to embarrass. Take heart love, she wouldn't have liked you regardless."

"I'm still here," his mother reminded them. Her mouth was pressed into a line so absolute her lips disappeared.

"Yes, you are." Austin glanced at her. "As I said, Kylie and I were just passing through. We can let ourselves out.

As if talking to a child, his mother heaved a delicate sigh, the only emotion she allowed herself, and tried again. "I know many suitable women, Austin. Yes, you've avoided any lasting relationship since that chit Delilah in college, but a man of your stature shouldn't stay single forever."

"My personal life is none of your business," Austin said quietly. Absently, he ran his thumb along Kylie's wrist. "In fact, nothing about me concerns you. Tend to your husband's concerns. He requires your attention far more than I do."

This comment got the reaction it sought. Brinkley's nose flared. Her eyes narrowed on her son but when she spoke, her voice betrayed no irritation or avarice.

"I beg to differ," she said studying the obscenely large diamond on her left hand. "Who you choose to associate with reflects on me. This slovenly, disheveled excuse for a woman is not a proper acquaintance for daylight hours. She's meant for darkness and closed doors, not for parading around where anyone might mistake her for more than she is."

"Hey!" Kylie startled the combatants. "Don't talk about me like that!" She said, getting up and advancing on the woman. "I understand that you crave your son's attention and because you lack positive social skills, you don't know any way to get it besides to stab him with words to see if he bleeds. Recognize that I'm not a relative of yours. If you insult me, I will take it personally."

"My goodness, dear." Brinkley put a hand to her chest with fingers raised. "What do you plan to do to me? Beat politeness into me?"

"No," Kylie said facing the woman. "If you say words to hurt me I might perhaps retaliate in kind. I might say that your son doesn't see it, but you are so fragile and brittle that you could shatter at a word of genuine kindness. That you crave your son's attention but fear if you make an overture, it may result in rejection. I could say that no one has loved you in your life, but you have longed for the emotion from the moment you first drew breath. I could say…"

"Enough!" Brinkley said cutting the tirade short. "None of that is true so it has no effect on me," she said with resolve. However, catching the wide eyes of her son, she couldn't hold his gaze and turned away. "All I'm saying is for your own good. Don't get attached to Austin. He will never keep you."

"Duly noted, Ms. DeAngelis, but I'm not trying to keep Austin. I'm only using him for sex." Kylie ignored Austin's bray of laughter behind her. Looking at him, she motioned towards the door. "Austin, as entertaining as all this has been, can we go? Your mother has enjoyed our company long enough." She turned back to the older woman and said almost kindly. "A word of advice, if you tried being warmer to him maybe he would return less periodically." The comment was met with a blank stare. Kylie shrugged and made for the door. "Austin, are you coming? The desperate longing in this room is stifling."

Seeming to snap out of a trance, Austin followed behind her. Almost out the door, it seemed he couldn't help throwing a last look at his mother. She stared out at the darkening view through the window.

"Is any of that true, Mother?" The question was asked with a hint of hope that anyone with ears could detect.

"Austin, don't be ridiculous," she snapped. "If I wanted or needed your affection you would have given it to me with little effort years ago. You've always been so needy." With that, she seemed to dismiss him from her thoughts.

In response, Austin slowly and carefully closed the door behind them, leaving his mother alone as she preferred.

Chapter Eleven

"What the hell was that?" Kylie finally demanded, voicing the words that had been locked behind her teeth through the long, silent car ride from his mother's house.

Austin was clearly uncomfortable. "What?" he asked avoiding her eyes. He walked into her studio, moved to her bed, and sat with his elbows resting on his knees. "You asked me about my mother." He explained studying his fingers. "I wanted you to meet her. You wouldn't have agreed to go if I told you that's where we were going."

"You're damn right I wouldn't have agreed. Why?" she questioned again.

He shrugged. "I want you to know me," he said. The words were flat but conveyed some emotion that made Kylie's breath catch. "Meeting her was the best way to explain to you who and what I am."

STEFANIE GRAHAM

"Austin, look," she said moving to sit beside him. She hesitated a minute before she reluctantly but resolutely took his hands in hers. "We barely know each other, but even I can tell that woman is not responsible for the man you are. She couldn't be. Someone loved you and showed you some compassion while you were young. If that wasn't true, you wouldn't have been able to show that compassion to me."

He said nothing.

Kylie got up and started pacing. She had so much she wanted to know following that introduction, but she realized that they were navigating dangerous waters. They were crossing from fuck buddies to something else, something unknown. She didn't know if she was ready to know Austin beyond the superficial. If she did, she knew there would be no way for her to keep herself separate. In the end, lack of self-preservation and lurid curiosity won out.

"Tell me about the chit Delilah from college?" she said, partially quoting his mother's words.

"Who?" Austin pretended ignorance.

Instead of answering, Kylie pinned him with a look.

Austin sighed. "I'd rather not talk about a time in my life when I was stupid and naive. It doesn't bring back good memories."

"*I want you to know me.*"Those were your words," Kylie reminded him. "I'm happy to go on as we were — more than happy. I barely know what we're even doing crossing lines that don't need crossing anyway. You're the one that opened that door. Step in or step out!"

Everything on Austin was stiff, tense and unmoving, as he visibly struggled with himself. Kylie took pity on him.

"Forget I asked," she relented. "This is obviously a difficult subject. I'm not exactly the most forthcoming person in the world, so I know how you feel."

Different emotions played across Austin's face until finally he looked at her and said, "Where do you want me to start?"

Kylie's response was simple. "Start wherever feels right."

Austin could already feel the tension building in his shoulders. Kylie meant something to him and if recalling one of the rather more humiliating times of his life would make her feel closer to him, then he would do what it took. He wanted her to depend on him and to trust him, but that meant he had to trust her. It was a good strategy in theory, but reminiscing brought with it that sick feeling in his stomach that he hadn't felt in years. He'd so eradicated the foolish boy he'd been from his mind, that just thinking of the poor, pathetic youngster he'd been, made his insides burn with a combination of mortification and shame.

"There once was a boy from Bridle Path, Toronto who went to school at U of T." Smiling, Austin began his tale in a sing-song voice.

"Cut it out!" Kylie warned.

The smile fell away almost instantly. Sweat broke out on Austin's upper lip. His hands felt damp and he wiped his palms against his pants.

"Two women in my life have made a lasting impression on me." He began again. "One is my mother, who you've had the misfortune of meeting. The other is Delilah Acevedo. Delilah was my college sweetheart. I met her at freshman orientation and fell instantly and insanely in love with her...I thought. She was everything I'd dreamed about in a woman. She had a seductive innocence about her that drove me wild. I wanted her like I had never wanted anything before.

"Our *love* was complicated from the beginning. I'd never really let anyone close to me, but I wanted to spend every waking hour in Lilah's company. She told me she felt the same, but there was a catch. Delilah was a strict Catholic, and a virgin. I was a raving machine of lust. I wanted her in every way I could have her, but Lilah kept me at arm's length. It was a masterful strategy. Her mercurial moods, her teasing, and her protestations of love while keeping me away, drove me deeper under her spell.

"I understood her reluctance. She'd felt me once when I pressed myself against her and knew it wouldn't be easy. So, I coaxed her into cooperation for close to a year. Months and months of using my tongue, my hands, and my teeth, anything to bring Lilah pleasure so she'd know she had nothing to fear from me. I'd be easy, gentle, and loving. After all, I didn't know how to be anything else. I'd learned early that women were breakable, delicate, and they could be hurt if not handled with care.

"No woman had anything to fear from me. Lilah, who'd I shared every secret of my soul with, knew all about that. She used that knowledge against me. She said I had to wait. *I had to give her time. She was so scared. Couldn't we just wait?* My answer each time was yes. I would have waited a lifetime if she had asked me to. By the time I became impatient, we'd been dating for months; I'd given her a million presents. I'd done everything a man could do to coax Lilah into letting me make love to her."

"What happened?" Kylie asked. Her expression appeared carefully neutral even though she couldn't hide the pity in her eyes.

With difficulty, Austin made his mind drift back to when he was eighteen. He hated doing it. It made him angry

STEFANIE GRAHAM

and when he was angry, he needed an outlet for his aggression. That wouldn't happen today and it made him even more furious. He turned away from Kylie and stalked to the window. He dug his hands into his pockets and looked out at the scenery before speaking.

"I thought I loved her and was convinced she loved me. I took the utmost care when she finally told me yes, as if I'd been given a gift from God. I peeled off her clothes like she was created just for me. I felt honored you see, nervous if I'm honest. Can you believe that?" He laughed harshly without looking at Kylie. "*Me*. Nervous? At eighteen, what I'd lacked in years of experience, I made up for in imagination and creativity. I had studied every part of the female body. I was a student of carnality and control. It took a strong will to say no to all the women on campus that were determined to give me everything. I'd mastered myself for the most part. I had self-control and discipline but I still worried that I would be rushed, hurried, and impatient; that my greed would make me hurt the one person I cared about. I was faithful to Lilah, chaste even. It was cute really, in an excruciatingly humiliating way."

Austin turned away from the view and then looked directly at Kylie. His gaze was harsh — penetrating. "It was like a gift when she finally gave in to me. When I entered her, Delilah cried out and then started with real tears. Her

144

anguish was so believable that I felt guilty for demanding this one small demonstration of her love for me after months and months of waiting. I lasted minutes, and was so enamored by my success that I didn't notice that my virgin girlfriend didn't have any difficulty at all accepting all of me."

Kylie got up and moved towards him. "Austin," she said running her hands along his arm that tensed into steel at her touch, "you don't have to tell me anymore. I get it. I'm sorry I asked about her; it's obviously a terrible memory for you."

"Terrible?" Although Austin repeated her words, his mind was elsewhere. "Terrible, yes, but you wanted to hear about my past, so I'll tell you. She was a virgin." His mouth twisted wryly. "And after almost a year of waiting, I was as near a virgin as a man could be. She was innocent and sweet, and I was a monster for not making the emotional love we shared enough to satisfy me. Blessedly, thankfully, it was over quickly, and I was happy, very happy for the first time in my life. My girl had survived a session with me and it would only get better from there. I was so excited that we had crossed this hurdle. I could barely keep my happiness contained.

"The next day I skipped all my classes and went to Delilah's dorm room and burst in without knocking. What I saw nearly stopped my heart. I know what it feels like to suffocate; how it feels not to be able to breathe. There she was, the girl I thought was virginal up until recently, naked and very busy with two of the biggest and burliest members of the football team.

"Stretched out on the bed between them, she looked like an angel being ravished by devils to me. It was an illusion. How else could I explain that the world seemed to have tilted on its axis and was spinning? I sank down on my knees on the floor. The laughter was what cleared my head — laughter at my expense. The footballers took pleasure in telling me how many times and how often they'd shared my girlfriend between them while I went around with blue balls. Delilah, the woman I loved, was a liar and a world-class bitch and I was the gullible fool who she'd suckered into loving her and buying her gifts. If I could have gotten my hands on her I still don't know what I would have been capable of doing. Luckily for her, the scars of my childhood and the habits of a lifetime stuck. I don't hurt women. Not physically, but had I touched her that day I would have hurt her. I believe if I saw her again, even now, I still could."

"I'm sorry, Austin." The look on Kylie's face suggested she bitterly regretted having started this. She looked at him, eyes filled with compassion for the boy he was.

"Don't feel sorry for me," he growled feeling the muscles in his jaw clench.

"I don't." Kylie protested. "I feel sorry for her. She lost you. She didn't know what she had."

"Yes, I'm an incredible prize," he said denying her claim.

She walked up to him and gently rested her hand along his clenched jaw. "You are incredible."

He grabbed her delicate wrist and squeezed. Not hard but with enough pressure to make a normal woman nervous.

"I'm not in the mood for gentleness now, Kylie. Let's not do this right now."

"Now is the perfect time," she insisted.

"No, it's not. I'm feeling violent and angry. Old memories make me want to hurt something and someone. I'm not fit company. Let me work this out at the gym and then we will talk."

Kylie shook her head and wiggled her wrist until he released his grip. When she was free, her hands went immediately to the zipper holding her top together.

"Don't," Austin snapped.

"You said you're feeling aggressive — no need for the gym. I'm here. Work off your aggression on me." There was lust burning in her eyes.

Austin took in a deep breath. "You don't know what you're asking. Are you crazy! I could hurt you, badly." He turned his back to her.

Naked to the waist, Kylie pressed her breasts into Austin's back and wrapped her arms around him. He went rigid all over and it excited her. His discipline. His restraint. She wanted to break his control. In that moment, it was as if she had spent her whole life not wanting anything else.

"Let go!" he commanded, his voice a soft growl. Disobedient by nature, Kylie did the opposite. She spun him around, unraveled his scarf from his neck, peeled his jacket from his body, then grabbed a fistful of his shirt in her hands, and ripped it open.

Buttons went flying.

Satisfaction spread through Kylie as they flew upwards and scattered. With a smile on her lips, she watched Austin's breathing grow ragged as he fought with himself. His light green eyes glowed. Only the rising and falling of his chest gave any indication of his turmoil. He was a master at this. She wasn't, but she was learning. Determined to provoke him, she massaged his chest. She took his dark, dusky nipples between her fingertips and squeezed...hard. His breath burst from his lips, but he remained immobile.

"You're playing with fire, little girl," he told her. His lips pressed into a solid line.

Kylie continued. "You know, I've always found it a terrible shame that most women neglect the male nipple. If we like your hands, lips, and teeth on our nipples, doesn't it stand to reason that men would like it too? You, sir, have some exceptional pectorals. They look good, they feel good, and oh wait, do they taste good?" she asked keeping eye contact. "Let's see." She proceeded to wrap her lips around his nipple while sucking it into her mouth.

Austin drew in a breath and his hands reached up and tangled in her hair. He held her that way as her tongue circled his nipples. He didn't pull her closer but didn't push her away. He accepted her ministrations serenely until Kylie grazed the underside of his nipple with her teeth. That set off an explosion in him. His hands tightened in her hair until Kylie's scalp protested the rough treatment. He grabbed her from the underside of her arms and lifted her off her feet.

"No more," he said again.

"Austin," Kylie licked her lips. "In case you didn't realize, you are not the boss of me. Take it like a man, you're about to get pistol-whipped." With that, Kylie pushed against him hard, catching him enough by surprise that his back slammed against the wall behind them. Kylie launched herself against him, her hands, lips, and teeth everywhere. What her practiced torture couldn't accomplish, her wildness did. Austin had had enough it seemed. He picked her up as if she weighed nothing, tugged her leggings from her body and, with one heave, lifted her high above his head. To keep her balance, she was forced to grab a fistful of his hair in her hands and wrap her legs around his neck for balance. He had her right where he wanted her. She realized her danger immediately and tried to scramble down. Austin eased his head back just as she looked down at him.

"Now look what kind of trouble you're in," he uttered. All evidence of anger was gone. He stroked his hands down the cheeks of her ass before he leaned forward and buried his head between her legs.

Kylie gasped and then groaned as Austin licked past the mesh of her panties. In this position, she was as vulnerable as she'd ever been. Her pussy was pressed firmly and securely against Austin's greedy mouth. He took full advantage. He inhaled and pushed his nose against her clit before raising his head and sucking the bud into his mouth. Without warning, Kylie climaxed. Only then did Austin lift her off his shoulders and set her on wobbly feet.

"I will not be rushed or provoked into hard, quick fuck. I think there's been enough of that. Whether you like it or not, we are going to do this the way I want. The way I've dreamed about." With that, he scooped her up and flung her on the bed. Kylie bounced on the ultra-plush mattress before she settled.

"Austin, what if all I want from you is a hard, quick fuck?" She looked up at him from her sprawled position.

"That's too bad. We're going to try this my way." With that, Austin stood in front of her and methodically began taking off the rest of his clothes. He had to know what it did to women to see him naked. He had the body of an athlete, muscled and lean, without an inch of fat anywhere. The muscles were long, well-sculpted. In a suit, he could pass for a male model until he removed the clothes, showing what the suit hid. Her mouth went dry just watching him.

It was the first time she had to contend with sex with a man who looked better naked than she did. It was humbling really. She was short and petite. She grew up always yearning to be taller. Men liked that she was curvy but what woman didn't long for a few more inches that would make them at least average in height? She'd learned to love her small frame, but it had taken work.

Austin had almost discounted her as a bed partner because she was so small, but she had proved to him without a doubt that she could roll with the big girls. She could manage him in and out of bed and loved proving that to him. He was in for a lesson now.

"Take off the rest of your clothes!" he commanded.

"Make me," she said, further testing her limits. Instead of galvanizing him, Austin's mouth kicked into a half-grin.

"You'd like that, wouldn't you? You'd like me to rip off your underwear. I could do that, but I won't. Now be a good girl and take off your clothes for me...slowly, please."

"I'm yours to command," she said cheekily. She leaned back with her legs raised towards him and removed her panties. She took her time. All things pink and pouty teased him. She held up the strip of mesh she'd removed for his inspection. "All done," she said before tossing the panties to the floor.

Austin's mouth curved into a sensual slant. "...Indeed."

Chapter Twelve

Austin noticed the new security guard immediately. He couldn't say why the man caught his attention. He was sure he'd never laid eyes on him before, but still felt that the man's face should trigger a memory. This man didn't look like the typical security guard. Although his bearing carried hints of the military, as most of the men in his employ did, there was something insolent and predatory about the way he moved. There was a cockiness in the way he addressed the employees that walked through the door. There was arrogance in the way he interacted with them.

Austin saw all of this as soon as he walked through the door, but that wasn't what caught his attention. There was something vaguely familiar about the man. He felt like he knew or had seen him before. Staring at the man's bearded face and dark brown hair drew only a blank in his mind. Why then did he seem so familiar? Observing him from afar,

Austin noted that the dark eyes and the half-smile on his lips made him seem trustworthy and congenial. He had the kind of face that invited trust. He didn't like the new security guard for just that reason. Faces could be deceptive. They hid a multitude of sins. Those that ignored their instincts usually lived to regret it. If the man had something to hide, Austin would discover it. Those that thought they could deceive him did so at their own risk.

"Nathaniel, who's the new guard?" he asked his security director.

"Adrian Vanderline, sir. Is there a problem?"

Nathaniel looked concerned. Austin rushed to calm his fears. "No, there's no problem. He just seems familiar to me. Has he worked in any of my other buildings? Have I seen him before?"

"No sir, I'm reasonably sure that he's not a former employee. He's originally from New York. Most of his experience has been in various locations throughout the States. He was highly recommended by Beatrice in HR."

Austin furrowed his brow. "So, we ran a background check on him before we hired him, right?"

Nathaniel drew himself up with offended dignity. "...Of course, sir. No one gets a job here without passing a strict security screening. Your safety and that of your employees is very important to us. We would never let anyone work here without making sure they were legit."

"Yes, of course, Nathaniel. All the same, I like to personally meet all my employees. Call him over."

Adrian walked up to Austin with a smile on his face. "Hello, Mr. DeAngelis. It's nice to meet you. I've heard you're a hands-on employer, but I didn't think I'd get the pleasure of speaking with you directly. You have a great establishment here. I'm glad to be part of it." He shook Austin's hand firmly and stood waiting.

Austin blinked once. The greeting was perfect. It was enthusiastic with a hint of obsequiousness that was perfect for a man in his position. Somehow, Austin didn't think it was sincere. It was in his eyes. They were wide open and unblinking, almost innocent; at odds with law enforcement personnel much less a man of the military.

"Hello, Adrian. I understand that you were in the military?"

"Yes, two tours in Afghanistan and one in Kuwait. I worked mostly in IT. I stayed away from most of the action, but I was happy to serve my country. I got married and moved to the four one six. Now, I'm glad to serve my new country in other ways. Some people in my former life might think corporate security isn't much of a gig but I'm happy to do my part."

The answers were perfect, but something was off. Austin lived by his instincts. He was successful in business because he trusted his gut. His gut said something was off with the newest member of his security team.

"Well, welcome. It's nice to meet you," Austin said.

"Thanks, Mr. DeAngelis."

When Adrian left, Austin turned to Nathaniel. "Have Beatrice in HR run the check again," he said quietly. Let me know the results. We have a new product hitting the marketplace soon. We can't be too careful."

"Of course, Mr. DeAngelis," Nathaniel replied.

Austin nodded his head, satisfied. If Nathaniel thought he was crazy for insisting on another check, he didn't say so.

Kylie walked through the lobby's security checkpoint moments later with her head down. Her thoughts were immersed with her memories of her date with Austin and the delicious after-date night-cap. She barely registered the faces of the guards. They'd all tried to pick her up at one point or another and been rejected. Now they maintained a sullen truce, so she was aggravated when one of them stepped in her way and blocked her path.

"Excuse me. Can I pass?" she said without looking up.

"Sure, Ms. DeValle," the guard said in a syrupy-sweet tone.

"Ms. Derringer." She corrected him immediately and glanced up. Everything in her froze. It couldn't be, but it was — Soldier.

He stood in front of her grinning madly with his appearance disguised. "Surprised to see me?" His voice was low.

"What are you doing here?" Kylie demanded. Instantly, she looked around to see if anyone had noted their interaction.

"I'm working," he answered smoothly. His mouth curled in a smile that made the hair on the back of her neck stand up.

"Avion does high-end security checks and with your background, you'd never get the job," Kylie said trying to keep her voice even so she wouldn't betray the panic she felt inside.

"Well, I'm here," Soldier said. "How I got here is the least of your concerns. We'll be working closely together. I just wanted you to be aware that dear old dad has joined your work team."

"What do you want, Soldier?" she asked, taking in his beard and his brown contacts. She assumed the getup was his attempt to hide their resemblance to one another.

"Don't concern yourself just yet, Kylie. I'll explain everything later," he promised before walking off to join the security team at the desk. Kylie stared at him. He didn't turn back her way.

Kylie prayed that when her day was over, Soldier would have miraculously disappeared. She prayed that whatever get-rich scheme he had concocted this time wouldn't jeopardize her career. She should have known better. Out of uniform, a close-cropped beard covering the lower half of his face and a hat drawn low over his eyes, her father waited by her car. Ignoring him, she unlocked the door; attempting to get in quickly and drive off. However, the minute the locks released, he leaped into the passenger side. Kylie got in slowly and placed her hands, still clenching her keys, in her lap. Bracing herself, she turned to him reluctantly.

"What do you want, Soldier?" Kylie asked already dreading the answer. "You want something. You always want something. It can't be a coincidence that you're working here."

"...Coincidence? No." His smile showed his straight white teeth. Kylie knew that smile. It was the same smile he'd given her when he borrowed her allowance, when he flaked on outings, and when he failed to appear at crucial events in her life. There was never anything worthy behind that smile.

"Here's the thing," he said reaching over to grab the hand gripping the car keys. He pried her fingers opens, holding her hand as he spoke. "The minute I heard you worked here, I saw an opportunity. Sempia saw one too. It was an opportunity too good for Avion's biggest business rival to pass up. Something big is happening at Avion. In your position, you have access to the programmers and all their sensitive files and data. That's worth something," he said. The fake brown eyes gleamed.

"Wait, are you talking about corporate espionage?" Kylie interrupted in disbelief. "Why would a fortune 500 company take such a risk and why would they recruit you to spy on their competitor? You're hardly a spy."

"They didn't recruit me, darling. I volunteered," he said with pride. "That's the beauty of this entire thing, sweetie." He radiated excitement. "The plan, the risk, and the rewards are all mine. As the brainchild of this failsafe plan, I walked myself over to DeAngelis' biggest competitor, showed them my military credentials, and told them I was the answer to all their problems. They thought they'd have to spend millions hiring new aged hackers to breach firewalls. I told them I had someone who could slip right in. That person is you. Now you're going to be a good girl and make us very rich." He thrust a tiny device into her hand.

Kylie turned the tiny gadget over in her hand. "What's this?"

"This is a custom-made USB drive I got from my high-tech cohorts. It's highly illegal and highly effective. Find a way to insert it into any of DeAngelis' personal drives and the installed software will automatically copy everything."

"I won't!" Kylie said resolutely, thrusting the device back.

"You will," her father countered. "Let me tell you why. Your mother has a fight ahead of her. A possible medical emergency in the form of breast cancer, I believe. She was very talkative the last time we were alone together." The smile he gave her was sympathetic, but his eyes were cruel. "Imagine what would happen if you lost your job for stealing secrets and couldn't get another one because your reputation was destroyed? Why the prescription costs for oral chemotherapy medicine alone could leave a body damn-near destitute."

"You'd use my mother against me?" Kylie said without emotion, staring at the man who had given her life.

"I'm not using her against you, love." He gave her hand a comforting squeeze. "This deal I got cooked up can benefit us both. I'll split the take, provided of course that you do exactly what I say."

"If I'm caught, I could go to jail," she said, still trying to reason with him.

He smiled that beautiful smile that must have had legions of women trusting him with their hearts.

"Kylie, sweetie." His tone was condescending. "Jails are for people who get caught. You won't get caught. You're too smart and so am I."

"I'll just tell Austin what you're up to." She wanted to protect Austin. Needed to.

"Austin, is it?" Soldier said, his grin widening. "I didn't know you and the *boss* were on a first-name basis. Have you been giving him a little something on the side? I thought men like him had mistresses and leggy administrative assistants for that. I didn't think you would catch his eye in all your grunge wear." Soldier looked her over critically. "Not that I can blame him," he said at last, his assessment at an end. "The man is obviously a connoisseur. He has a great eye and could see past all the camouflage you use to see what I see. You, my darling daughter, are an exceptionally beautiful woman. I wonder how I can use this new development."

"You won't be using any aspect of my relationship with Austin against him or me. I won't do it."

"You won't?" Soldier's eyes gleamed. "Oh, I think you will," he said, grabbing her chin and squeezing until she cried out in pain. "Let me tell you why," he said when her gaze met his. "You will because if you don't, I will convince your boss that this scheme was your idea. Tell him that you got involved with him so you could get close enough to steal company secrets. He doesn't know you very well and I lie very convincingly."

"You wouldn't," Kylie whispered even though she knew instinctively that he would. Soldier didn't care about anyone, least of all her. She had spent her childhood, and a good part of her teen years, believing that he had at least a little love for her. Here, finally, was her proof. Soldier didn't care for her at all. "What exactly is your plan, David?"

Startled by the use of his first name, Soldier stared at her and understood by whatever he read in her expression, the change that had taken place. They were done. ...Finished. She was breaking all ties. Something wistful passed over his face but Kylie couldn't begin to guess what it was. She'd just lost a parent and this stranger was threatening her life and her budding relationship with Austin. She couldn't forgive him for that.

"It's simple really. Seduce him. Manipulate him. Figure something out," he said, all business. "I want the source data for this new product. Bring me whatever information you can get your hands on about what this product is and how it's made. As their technical writer, you'll have access to all their experts. I'm sure all those programming geeks will be more than happy to share their secrets with a pretty face. Gather as much intelligence as you can so we can get a decent picture of what they're making. Whatever we're missing, we'll just use your influence with your boss to complete the picture. It'll be easy."

"So, let me get this straight," Kylie said in disbelief. "You want me to commit corporate espionage. You then want me to prostitute myself to get any other miscellaneous data from my boss. Does that about sum it up?"

Soldier's smile was lecherous. "Don't whine, baby doll. I've seen your boss. It shouldn't be a hardship. You're sleeping with him anyway."

"With all this running around has it occurred to you that when the shit hits the fan, I'll be the first person they'll suspect?" She tried to inject reason into his crazy plan.

"It *has* occurred to me, Sweet, but I wouldn't worry about it. Your mom will have completed her treatment by then and she'll be healthy and happy. You'll have more money than you can count. You can take her and disappear to somewhere warm. She'd like that."

"You don't know what she'd like. What she'd like is to have her daughter not sitting in a Federal prison, but we've already discussed that. When is this fiasco slated to begin?"

He mussed her hair as if they'd just had a loving chat. "Cool your jets for now. I'll keep you posted. Now that I can tell the Sempia folks that you're all the way in, things should move quickly. Gather what intelligence you can in the meantime. I'll be in touch."

Her heart already heavy with heartbreak and despair, Kylie watched the man that used to be her father get out of her car and disappear. She was too upset to notice the intent bicycle messenger lounging against a nearby wall, idly smoking a cigarette. She was in so much trouble. What was she going to do now?

Chapter Thirteen

"What's up, brotha?"

Kinky raised a brow and raked his gaze over the bearded security guard in front of him. He only replied when the insolent perusal was done. "We brothers, man?" A frown knitted his brow. "I wonder why my mother never told me? Here I have a long-lost brother, white at that, and dear old mama never said a thing!"

The guard's expression turned mean. "What can I do for you?" He stepped from behind the security desk and into Kinky's personal space. "Somehow, I think you might have lost your way, *brotha*," he emphasized. "I very much doubt that you have any business in this building." All pretense of conviviality vanished as he took in Kinky's well-worn Air Jordan's, skinny jeans, and slogan *We The North* Raptors t-shirt.

"How you figure?" Kinky said, drawing himself up to his full height. "You just took one look at me and decided I don't belong? And for the record, *brotha*...," he said, stressing the word, "you don't look like you belong here yourself. As a matter of fact," he continued, "against these straight-laced, zipped-up, conservative fellows, you look out of place." At the guard's startled look, Kinky continued unfazed. "I have business in this building here, so why don't you call up to the top floor, so I can get moving. I loved our little family reunion, but I have things to do and people to see."

They eyed each other distrustfully for a few seconds before the guard stepped away and went to the desk to make the call. He glared at Kinky, who leaned his full weight against the desk and snapped his gum.

"You're cleared. It's the last elevator on your left. It's the top floor."

"I know where I am going, cadet. And the next time you see me, I'd like a *sir* or a *mister* when you address me. You dig, bro?"

The guard didn't hide his burning resentment.

"Something ain't right with one of your cadet's downstairs," Kinky said, breezing into Austin's office unannounced. Outside the door, his newly hired receptionist looked like she was about to call in the National Guard. Austin waved her back to her seat just as she looked ready to go into hysterics. Inwardly, Austin was smiling. He knew Kinky as mild-mannered and convivial, but to the eye, he looked imposing. It wasn't just his size or the obvious discrimination that came with his color and his clothing. He just looked...hard. Breezing by his assistant, Kinky probably had conjured thoughts of Austin being assaulted in some interoffice incident. It wouldn't occur to her, or anybody else, that he and Kinky could be friends.

"What is this about the people downstairs?" Austin decided not to bother reprimanding Kinky for coming by unannounced and scaring his staff. There was no point; he'd just do it again.

"One of your security and I had a little chat," he said pacing around the office. "I think this particular guy has been around. I've seen a thousand tricksters and con men in my life, and if that one is military and cop qualified, I'll go join the force myself."

"Which guard?" Austin asked. He already knew. He had the same feeling but had been reassured by the head of security that all the staff was gold-star material. The extensive screening a guard had to pass to get the job ensured their qualifications. But Kinky was right. Austin felt it too.

"The cocky, brown-eyed one," Kinky stated. "I'm gonna keep an eye on him. ...Check him out for you," he announced.

"No, no, that's alright," Austin said hastily envisioning Kinky behind bars if he decided to investigate the background of a military man. "I've got it covered."

Kinky looked skeptical but didn't say anything else. Instead, he said, "I'm here for that dinner you promised me. I'm starved." Kinky looked at his watch, "It's going on four o'clock. I don't like eating anytime past seven. Can you be ready to go by then, man? Don't tell me you need reservations, or you can't go *cause you got plans*. I aim to spend some quality time and I'm thinking you should agree."

It sounded almost threatening. Austin resisted the urge to laugh in Kinky's face. He did have plans and liked reservations but he gave in without a fight. He didn't have friends; he had coworkers, acquaintances, and girls who dropped by for fun. He could do with some relaxation with someone who not only expected him to be himself but demanded it. "How does McDonald's sound — a Big Mac?"

"Brotha, you crazy. I don't eat that shit." Kinky sounded truly scandalized. "It's bad for my figure." He patted what appeared to be a six-pack. "I'm thinking Ruth's

Chris. I have a hankering for a bloody steak. I'll meet you there in two hours." Kinky left Austin's office without looking back.

With a narrowed gaze, Soldier watched as the man he'd tangled with earlier came out of the elevator. His steps slowed as he insolently strolled by the security desk. He took his time readjusting his messenger bag across his big body before heading for the front door. Before he exited, he had the audacity to look directly at him, smirk in derision and then wink. That did it. Call him petty and vengeful but no one, no one at all, crossed him. Any offense, big or small, came with a penalty. Before the day was over, the man would be sorry they'd met.

Soldier lifted the phone and quickly made a call.

"911. What is your emergency?"

"Yes, there's a suspicious black man outside the Avion Industries building. He has a bag that I believe may contain either a weapon or some contraband. I'm concerned for my safety. Please send help!"

Disconnecting, he dropped the business phone back into its cradle and smiled. *"If the police come and put that fool in a chokehold, then serve him right."* He said under his breath. No one crossed him. He just hoped his voice had carried the right mix of stranger danger and alarm.

Outside, the gleaming glass office building captured the soul of the city in its reflective surface. No sins could be hidden from a structure constructed of mirrored glass. Beauty and high-end luxury was the intention of the design, but a building made of glass has no choice but to reflect the truth of what it sees, even when what it sees is ugly."Get your hands off me! You have no right to detain me. I know my rights!" Austin heard the shouted words with what sounded like a violent scuffle just as he stepped out of the elevator. He had a phone conference in his car to complete before he met Kinky at the restaurant.

One of his security guards stepped from around the desk as he approached. "Mr. DeAngelis, can we take you around the side entrance to where your car awaits, sir? We redirected your driver from the front of the building. We have a police presence and a bit of unpleasantness happening outside."

Preoccupied with thoughts of his phone meeting, Austin veered towards the side entrance but the sound of a body hitting the concrete and yells from the front of his building halted him in his tracks. He stepped around his guard to investigate and was shocked by what he saw.

170

Kinky laid on the floor with an officer's knee in his back as the cop attempted to handcuff him. Yet another policeman had his hand around his neck, while a third tried to hold his flailing body to the ground.

"I didn't do anything wrong. This is racial profiling. I know my rights. Get the fuck off me!" Kinky swore still thrashing.

Austin was horrified. He stepped forward but a hand in his chest stopped him. "This is a police matter, sir. For your safety, please get back in the building. This man is under arrest."

"What's the charge?" Austin had to know.

"That's none of your concern, sir. Please return to the building," the officer said, his tone hard and uncompromising.

At that moment, Kinky's head was slammed against the concrete and still fighting the mistreatment; their eyes met from across the expanse. What he saw made his insides clench with an emotion he couldn't name. Kinky was a proud man. To be reduced to this squirming and battered heap on the ground at the mercy of others was excruciating. To have Austin witness his humiliation was worse still. He read the feelings of helplessness in the angry tears that Kinky refused to let fall.

Kinky was many things, but thief, thug or violent criminal, he was not. He'd bet his life on it.

He hit the speed dial button on his phone. "Meet me in the lobby this instant!" he told the person on the other end before he hung up and turned back to the officer. "I believe I have a right to know why you are arresting a person on my property, officer. I own this building. My security team is inside. If this man has done something illegal, then I need to be informed so I can assess whether I need to prosecute."

"Mr. DeAngelis. Sorry sir, I didn't recognize you." His tone became more respectful. "I'm Officer Jackson. This man is being arrested for criminal trespassing and possible possession of a firearm and drugs."

"I see," Austin said trying to keep the rage from his voice. "As I said, I own this building and this man is not and has not trespassed. He has legitimate business here. Have the weapon and drugs been found on his person then?" Austin's voice was deceptively soft.

"Not yet," The officer admitted with certainty in his tone. "But we'll find something. He has that look about him. You know the type."

"Oh yes, I do." Austin agreed as a young, pretty, biracial female in an outrageously expensive suit stopped beside him and the officer.

"Yes, Austin, I got here as fast as I could. What can I do for you?" she asked, her sharp and inquisitive gaze taking in the scene.

"Officer Jackson was explaining to me that my childhood friend on the ground here is suspected of wrongdoing. Apparently, based on his apparent criminal countenance, he's being arrested and charged. He needs representation."

He stepped around the protesting officer and walked to where Kinky lay bound. He had stopped struggling and lay still. Fury, fear and humiliation rolled off him in waves. Now was not a time for words. Instead, he turned to the other officers whose entire focus was now on him.

"This is Susan Sterling," he said pointing to the young woman. "She's my in-house council, and for the time being, Mr. Kincaid's attorney. Unless you've found a weapon or contraband on his person that we can all attest to seeing, I want him off the ground and uncuffed this instant. I'll leave it unsaid about what may have precipitated this arrest. I will let Susan handle matters there. Please be assured, however officers, that I plan to follow up on the outcome personally."

No one moved. "I said I want him off the ground now!" Austin's voice rose, the tone so cold and careful that it spurred the officers to action. Kinky was yanked from the floor to his feet. His breath came out with a hiss as the sockets of his arms protested further rough treatment.

Austin turned to Kinky, who was now rubbing the circulation back into his unbound wrists.

"I didn't do anything." He said to the floor, not meeting Austin's eyes. "Someone called the police on me. I'm out here trying to make an honest living and next thing I know, I'm face-down and in cuffs. This is the twenty-first century, right, 'cause this shit is getting old."

Austin couldn't find words so squeezed Kinky's shoulder instead. "Go home. Don't worry about this. Susan will take care of it. We respect our officers for doing their jobs, but if this was motivated by hatred and intolerance in any way..." Austin had to swallow past the emotion clogging his throat. "If this arrest was motivated by anything else besides protecting the public good, then they will have to answer to me."

Kinky's eyes met Austin's briefly. "Thanks, man. I owe you for this. This isn't the first time something like this has happened so I won't let them ruin my day or my dinner. Give me an extra hour. I still want to eat." He snatched his empty messenger bag from the floor, picked up the scattered mail and silently walked away with his head held high.

The dignity in which he held himself, despite his ripped clothes and now mangled messenger bag, made Austin swear softly.

The conference call would have to wait. "Officer Jackson," he called the man over. "Who made the call to the police?"

Sullen yet still solicitous, Jackson shrugged. "Not sure, sir, but the call originated from your building."

Austin nodded, troubled.

Austin showed up at the restaurant promptly. He'd decided to drive, so folded himself out of his Porsche 911, buttoned his tailored jacket, flicked off his sunglasses, and stood on the sidewalk with the setting sun gleaming down on his silver hair. To the onlooker, he looked like what he was, a rich, powerful man of means about to meet with a world leader or a captain of industry, so when the host caught sight of him; he began the routine spiel of falling over himself to make sure every one of Austin's needs was met.

"How can I help you, sir?"

"I have a reservation for two under DeAngelis. My secretary called a short while ago to secure the table. Sorry for the late notice and the time change but my friend really wanted to eat here."

"...Of course, Mr. DeAngelis. No problem. We're happy to accommodate you. We have our private dining room all set up. Is your friend here?"

Austin looked around. He didn't see Kinky anywhere in the restaurant so he glanced outside wondering if his earlier ordeal would lead to a no-show. He spied him walking around his 911 with his hands caressing the gleaming paintjob. He must have sensed Austin's scrutiny because he looked up as he came into the restaurant.

"Let me guess," he said walking up to Austin. "That orgasm on wheels is yours?"

"Yes," Austin said simply. "It's one of many. You think someone might beat me up and take it from me?" Austin said, trying to lighten the mood by jokingly referring to their shared past.

Kinky snorted at the jest. "I don't know, man," he said and gave the car another look. "I'd whip your ass for a lot less."

Neither of them mentioned the earlier incident. Both were content to pretend that nothing had happened.

They laughed awkwardly yet companionably but stopped abruptly when they noticed the look on the host's face. Taking their exchange seriously, he looked on the verge of calling the police...again. "We're just joking," Austin reassured him. "This is my dinner guest."

Frozen in place for half-a-second, the host looked to Kinky and back to Austin a few more times before he was able to speak.

"...to the food, man!" Kinky said his voice full of authority. "We don't got all day."

"...Of course, of course," the man said turning red. "Forgive me. This way, gentlemen." He led them inside the private dining room and Austin and Kincaid sat down. As soon as the host left, they looked at each other and laughed.

"Next time we meet, either I have to dress down or you have to dress up, so people can stop going crazy," Austin said. The laughter was still in his voice.

"Austin, my man, no disrespect, but you look expensive. No amount of Raptors jerseys will change that." They chuckled again, scanned their menus and ordered when the waiter came.

When the food arrived, Austin was surprised. He hadn't expected Kinky to balance delicately on a chair that looked minuscule beneath him, take the napkin the waiter offered him with the grace of a debutante, and lay it across his lap. Kinky then started in on his courses with the proper fork in hand.

As Austin watched him, transfixed, Kinky looked up. "What!" he said defiantly. "A brother can't have table manners? I watch YouTube. Proper etiquette is important.

Now stop staring at me like you demented and tell me about this hottie you have your eyes on. ...the little one, right? You think I didn't *peep* her when I came into your office. She didn't notice me, but a girl like that is hard to miss."

Austin didn't pretend to misunderstand. There was something about Kinky's bluntness that made people want to be forthright with him. Perhaps it was because he wasn't judgmental. When it came to people, he judged them based on their character alone. Austin lived in a world where people could care less about character. Instead, they were obsessed with your bank account, your watch, your stock portfolio, and the size of the rack on your woman. Kind hearts and good motives were weaknesses. That's probably why, besides Brix, Austin only had acquaintances and no real friends.

"She's twisting me inside out," Austin heard himself admit in shock. If he was a little less disciplined, he would have smacked his hand across his mouth. Where the hell did that admission come from? Playing back the words in his mind, he realized that they were true. He just hadn't allowed himself to admit them. He'd already given Kinky enough info to make a tabloid reporter happy, so he didn't bother to stem the flow of words. "There's just something about her that I can't seem to describe. She's aloof but giving, sensual but skittish. She's strong but seems fragile in so many ways. I want to capture her and hold her to me but every time I try, she pulls away. I don't know what it is about this girl that has me whipped, but she has a hold over me that I can't shake."

Kinky's fork froze halfway to his mouth. He slowly put it down and gave Austin his full attention. "Sounds like you got it bad, man. But I'd advise you to go slow. I like this one, but there is something about her that makes my eyes twitch." He made the declaration like he knew something Austin didn't

It was Austin's turn to freeze. "What? What is this about eye twitching?"

"I don't know," Kinky resumed eating, not willing or able to elaborate. "She seems like a lady with a lot on her mind. I wouldn't go so far as saying she's up to something, but something is definitely up. I suggest before you go all hearts and flowers on her, that you get to the bottom of what's bothering her."

"And you're assuming something's bothering her from your assessment from across the room?" Austin's voice chilled, his tone now a business mogul defending against a hostile takeover.

"Don't go all corporate-caveman on me." Kinky was immune to the change in the atmosphere. "I got a gut feeling and my gut is never wrong. *Trust.* But I see that you all *tight* right now and don't want to discuss your woman with the likes of me. Cool, no problem, man. Just remember what I said. You my man, even more so after what you did today; I only have your best interests at heart."

The words were spoken with rough sincerity. Austin relented and relaxed in his chair. "Sorry about that," he said, trying, and failing, to adopt a more casual tone. "Like I said, this one has me all tied up. I'll keep my eye on her just like you said."

"Good. I'll keep an eye on her as well," The assurance was made with a seriousness that Austin hadn't heard from Kinky before.

Austin didn't know why the conversation with Kincaid bothered him. It probably had to do with the fact that something about what he said resonated with him. Kylie was off; her mood was unpredictable. She was obviously struggling with something but didn't trust him enough to share it. He wanted her to trust him and wanted her to rely on him to make all her worries go away. That he might only be an entertaining bed partner to her didn't sit well with him. Suddenly, for the first time in his life, he wanted to be, *needed* to be...more.

Chapter Fourteen

"This is for you." Without explanation, Austin thrust the small, elaborately wrapped box into Kylie's hand.

Not used to presents of any kind, she tried to contain the smile that threatened to split her face. She shook the box and put her ear to it, so she could hear if it rattled. She reverently caressed the hot pink wrapping paper and ran her fingertips over the black skull and crossbones ribbon. The wrapping was a combination of girliness and Goth — a perfect representation of who she was. She loved it without having to open the box to see what was inside. Suddenly, out of nowhere, she felt pressure building behind her eyes. A scratchy feeling clogged her throat. Holy hell she thought, was she going to cry? Not if she could help it. She turned away momentarily, attempting to pull herself together. She turned back to meet Austin's eyes when she felt more in control. "I love it, Austin. Thank you."

She would have preferred that her tone be light and flippant, but she couldn't manage it. The gift meant too much to her for her to pretend that the gesture was insignificant. No one had given her a gift since she was eight years old; old enough to know that there was no Santa Claus. Once the illusion had been shattered, her mother who'd always struggled with money didn't see the necessity to continue the pretense. She bought her things, new things and things she wanted, but they were either thrust in her hand without being wrapped or left on her bed long after the significant date, birthdays and holidays, had passed.

For that reason, the fact that Austin had unwittingly taken the time to buy her a gift, wrap it, and hand it to her as a true surprise made her emotional. She placed the gift on her desk. They were alone together in her cubicle with everyone having gone home for the day. She glanced at the package again. With Soldier's threats hanging over her head, she felt both guilty and grateful. She hated the feelings, so she pushed them to the back of her mind.

"Aren't you going to open it?" Austin asked like an impatient child. He snatched the package off her desk and dropped it back into her hands. "I want you to open it now. I want to see your face."

Kylie was almost afraid to open it. She wanted to be alone when she did. No matter what was inside the package, which she was sure was something tasteful and expensive, possibly as extravagant as the man himself, too much emotion in front of Austin would give him ideas. He might think she loved him or that she cared. Under the circumstance, both revelations would be disastrous. As far as Austin was concerned, all he needed to know was that she liked his body, his mouth, and all the wonderful things he could do with both. Any further sentiment could be ruinous for them both.

Watching her internal struggle, Austin snatched the package from her hand and deliberately ripped it open, destroying the pretty pink paper. Taking the string, he wrapped it around her wrist and then placed the box no bigger than a cigar case, in her hand.

"The hard part is over. Open the damn box!" It was a command said with exasperation pushed past its limits. Smiling, Kylie did what she was told and opened the box. The smile left her face abruptly. Blinking, her eyelashes fluttering to fight back a rush of emotion, she stared down into the contents of the box. Her throat was too clogged for speech.

"Do you like it?" Austin asked. His voice was soft with something that in another man would have been taken for trepidation. "You're different, unconventional, and very difficult to shop for. The usual just didn't seem appropriate. Getting jewelry just didn't seem like the thing to do. Knowing your taste, I would have gotten that all wrong anyway, so I took a chance and got you this. I wanted you to like it. I understand if you don't. I had it inscribed with your initials and everything, but don't let that bother you if it isn't your thing. They'd take it back if I insisted." Austin stuttered to a stop, realizing he'd been rambling.

Kylie still hadn't said anything. She lightly stroked the contents of the box. When she looked up at Austin, her eyes must have appeared stricken.

Austin snatched the box from her hand. "It was stupid. You probably don't like this kind of stuff. Who gives this kind of gift to a woman anyway?"

Startled, Kylie snatched the box back. "Austin...," she trailed off not knowing what to say. She tried again. "This is the best gift anyone has ever given me. It's even better than the wrapping paper."

Austin let out a startled laugh. "So you like it. It wasn't a mistake?"

"No," she said looking at him. "It's perfect. She reached into the box and palmed the antique 357 double-barrel Lady Derringer. It had an ivory handle with a scantily clad Victorian woman on the grip. The rest of the gun was composed of polished steel. The pistol gleamed in her hand. Made to house just two shots, the gun was small. The steel was hard, but its beauty surpassed all imagining. Was this how he saw her? The thought that must have gone into the gift boggled her mind. Derringers were collector's items. Just how much had the gun cost? She wanted to ask but couldn't. If the cost was exorbitant, she'd be moved to give it back. She loved it too much to do that.

"I'll treasure it always, Austin. Thank you." She couldn't say more. Not if she wanted to avoid dissolving into a blubbering mess in front of him. Austin exhaled, grinning from ear-to-ear.

"I nailed it, didn't I?" he said full of confidence and bravado now that the tense moment had passed. "Don't think that we're done here. We're going to the range baby-girl. I want to see your skills. I'll weep real tears if you have a name like Derringer and can't shoot worth a damn."

"Can't shoot?" Kylie looked at him with pity. "If you can find a range at this hour, I'd be happy to show you."

Kylie was tiny. The barrel of the rifle seemed to overpower her small frame, but she held it like a pro. Head cocked to the side, safety goggles on and protectors over her ears, she studied the target for a second before pulling the trigger with a series of rapid clicks. Her fingers danced over the trigger with elegant little twitches. She made it look effortless and easy.

Austin expected the target to resemble a riddled, off-kilter mess. His own target showed a respectful spattering of holes, most of them near the center-mass of the target. Kylie could only hope to do better. He decided he would be magnanimous about it and not tease her too cruelly. He waited as she pressed the button that brought her target within eyesight. To his shock, the holes were all head and heart. There were no stray bullet holes anywhere.

"Ah hell," Austin's mouth twisted into a grimace.

Kylie turned to him, smiling widely. "What did you expect? Shooting is the one good thing my father ever taught me," her smile dimmed at some memory but lit up again. "With a name like *Derringer*, I had to live up to my moniker or die of shame," she said with obvious delight.

"You're a goddamn sniper is what you are!" Austin said, snatching her target from the conveyer. He shook his head and pulled the protector from her ears. "Most girls like dinner and a movie." He bent down to kiss her lips.

"I'm not most girls," Kylie replied decisively.

She was right. She was different, and that difference meant everything.

They ended up at his house. Kylie insisted she wanted to *thank him* properly for her gift. It wasn't an invitation he was prepared to refuse. He kept on telling himself that if he wanted them to be more than fuck-buddies, they had to spend more time outside of the bedroom. The only problem was that the bed was where they were happiest. They were good together between the sheets; as good as two people could be.

Austin gripped Kylie by her throat from behind and pulled her body against his so her limbs were plastered to his from back to thigh.

"Yes!" Kylie breathed, every part of her softening and surrendering to his forceful grip.

"Is this what you want, Kylie?" Austin whispered into her ear.

"Yes, please ... Yes!" She exclaimed gyrating her ass against his huge cock.

Austin pulled Kylie's neck back further, exposing her vulnerable throat to his lips. He trailed kisses down the column of her neck, nipping and biting in the places that he liked best. Kylie ground herself against his erection.

"Take me just like this, Austin. Take me from behind!" she demanded.

Austin pushed her head down so that she bent at the waist with her behind jutting out in perfect position for an invasion. It aroused him to see Kylie's hair skimming the floor, to see her shirt climbing up her waist to expose her midriff. It aroused him that she liked him to ride her hard and put her away wet. But, in the deepest recesses of his heart, Austin longed for her to want him not as a stud for hire but as something more, something else. So, despite part of him screaming for release, he lifted her up and gently set her away from him.

"How about we watch TV, or a movie or something?" Austin suggested through gritted teeth. It nearly killed him.

It was obvious from the look she gave him that Kylie hadn't registered what he'd said. When she did, her eyes narrowed, and a wild look entered her eyes. However, when she spoke, the words that came out were calm.

"What's the matter, Austin? Don't you want to fuck me?"

"Fuck you?" Austin said, crawling need twisting his lips. "Yes, I want to fuck you. Is that all there is to this? I'm not complaining, but there's a problem if the only way you can enjoy sex is when it's explosive and angry. Good sex and making love can include being gentle."

"How do you know what making love is like, Austin?" Kylie challenged. She was visibly stung by the implication she was abnormal in some way. "Have you been in love before? *Making love* as you put it, if that is what we're doing, is any way we choose to do it. Rough, gently, standing up or lying down. There are no rules for how love makes you feel. Am I too aggressive for you?" she challenged. "If I am, it's because

I'm under control in every other aspect of my life. In the bedroom, I want passion and violent emotion tempered by moments of sweetness and calm. That's the way you make me feel. I want to devour you. I want you to devour me. I want to wrench every drop of passion out of you and then start all over again. I'm violently attracted to you and the violence in me responds to the violence in you. Why are you fighting it?"

Austin looked away. "...Because I want you to want the real Austin. All of me, not just the part that makes you scream."

Kylie casually walked towards him and put her hands on his erection. "You mean this part?"

"Yes," he said through gritted teeth before stepping back and out of reach.

Kylie was undeterred. She stepped close to him again and held his gaze. "Austin, have I ever told you that I think that you're beautiful."

"No," Austin said laughing, "You never have. I think that's what I'm supposed to say to you."

"I haven't told you because I know women throw themselves at you. You must have heard those words a million times before."

"I haven't," Austin said still staring at her. "And even if I had, it would sound different coming from you."

"Well, I think you're beautiful. More beautiful than I am, which is a bit disconcerting." At his snort of laughter, she went on. "I like that your hair is like liquid silver and I like the way it highlights your bronze skin. All day, every day, at work, all I do is dream about running my fingers through it and pulling...hard. I want you to know that I love your eyes. I've never seen green that color before. They are too bright and beautiful to describe. They are like jade mixed with the color of the sea. Looking at them sometimes makes it hard for me to concentrate."

"Why are you telling me this?" Austin asked. He was mesmerized by her words.

"I'm telling you this because I want you to know that you have a hold on me. I want to fight it, and you, but I can't. You have a beautiful body and I want all of it. I'm naturally cautious about everything and everyone, but with you, I'm free to explore everything that scares me because I trust you. I shouldn't, but I do. The sex is exceptional, Austin, but it's not the only reason I'm drawn to you. I'm drawn to you because I can be myself, quirky and moody without having to apologize or explain. It's refreshing. It's intoxicating and I want more. Can I have some more, Austin?"

He didn't even think about it. "Yes, come here."

She went to him immediately, but she shook her head and stepped to the side when he moved to put his arms around her. At his expression of confusion, she explained.

"Let me show you that I can be gentle too." With that, she fell to her knees, put her hands on the fly of his pants and started to unzip them. The part of Austin she said she cherished sprung free. As always, it was an impressive sight. She was a small woman, so she needed two hands to grip him successfully. Her grip was firm but then she softened her touch. Austin leaned forward giving her silent encouragement. Kylie kept her touch light. She circled the head of his penis with soft strokes. When the liquid formed on the tip, she touched it with her finger and put the finger in her mouth. Austin groaned. Lightly, she began stroking him. Gently, she put her mouth on him and began slowly sucking him.

"...More, harder, now!" Austin fired the commands through bared teeth but Kylie ignored him. She wrapped her lips around the head of his cock and drew him into the warm cavern of her mouth. She took her time going down the shaft.

Austin grabbed her hair, urging her to increase her rhythm. He wrapped his hands around hers and directed her on how to stroke him with more force.

"Tsk, tsk, tsk, Mr. DeAngelis, now stop that," she commanded, releasing him. "You said you wanted gentle. Gentle is what you'll get."

"Fuck that!" Austin said. In one swift movement, he grabbed her by her armpits and lifted her to eye-level. She had no choice but to wrap her legs around his waist.

"You said you wanted it gentle," Kylie reminded him. "I don't want to exploit you."

"I've decided gentleness is overrated," Austin said staring into her eyes just as he pushed his dick, full hilt, inside the moist cavern of her body.

Kylie's head fell back. "Yes." She breathed as ecstasy took hold.

Austin groaned. "*Yes,* is fucking right," he agreed.

Chapter Fifteen

"I spoke to the doctor. He wants to operate immediately." Her mother's voice on the phone sucked the air from the room. Naked, Kylie got up from the bed, put on one of Austin's pajama tops, and walked over to the window to take in a view she could no longer see.

"They prescribed a chemotherapy drug that they believe in for women like me, but it's not covered by insurance. I don't have the money. The cost is going to bankrupt me, Kylie." Her mother's voice rose with panic.

"Let me worry about that," Kylie said softly. Her mind was already in overdrive. "Kylie." Her name on her mother's lips expressed all her fears.

"Don't be afraid. We'll get through this together." Kylie attempted to convey confidence she didn't feel.

"Yes, we will," her mother agreed. Her voice choked with tears. "I'm so grateful for you. I know you don't want to hear this, but I'm grateful for your father too. I don't know why, but when I heard the news, he was the first person I called. Do you know what he said, Kylie?"

Kylie's grip tightened on the phone and her other hand balled into a fist. "What? What did he say, Mom?" She already dreaded the answer.

"He said that he had some money coming to him." Her voice rose with hope. "He said that money belonged to you for all the years of support he owed us. Can you believe it, Ky? I know you've never believed it, but he's a good man."

"Yeah, good," Kylie agreed, remembering that the USB he'd given her was still in her purse. She marched over to her bag and rummaged through it until she palmed the device in her hand. She wanted to hurl it across the room. *It'll be easy.* Easy, her father had said. Kylie shook her head and gripped the phone tighter. How could stealing from a man who guarded his privacy so religiously be considered easy? Yet when her father had given her the device to complete her larceny, he'd described the task as easy...

Easy for who — easy how?

"Seduce him. Manipulate him. You're my daughter and way more than just a pretty face, figure something out!" She tried shaking off the memory of his unreasonable demands, but it kept repeating in her head. *"You're going to get this done and done quickly. If the competitors don't get those files*

soon, they'll be of no use. Figure it out, Kylie. Your mother's life depends on it!"

Yeah, her father was a *good* man. Kylie covered her face with her hands and willed herself not to give in to the urge to cry hysterically.

Austin awoke to the sound of sniffling. Frowning, he glanced at his bedside clock. It was just after four in the morning. Sitting up, he was surprised to see Kylie standing across the room, speaking softly into her phone.

"Don't worry. I'll take care of everything. You just focus on getting better." She ran a hand through her hair, and when she turned, he saw that tears wet her cheeks.

He must have made a noise because she jumped then said softly, "I have to go." She avoided his gaze and closed her fist around something in her hand. When she returned to bed, her hands were empty, cheeks dry and her gaze almost defiant, as if daring him to comment.

Austin was never one to back down from a challenge. "Tell me what's wrong."

"Nothing. I mean, it's just my mom. We're both having a hard time with the cancer diagnosis."

Austin wanted to believe her. But his gut had been twisting for a while, and he couldn't let this go. Something was up with Kylie. Had been for a while. He grasped her hand, keeping her from bolting from the bed.

"I'm not trying to upset you. You just seem...off. Like something is on your mind." *I'm worried about you.* He swallowed the words, not wanting her to accuse him of going soft again.

Some of the tension leaked from her posture, and she smiled. "Nothing is on my mind except one thing, Austin. What do you say to some before sunrise breakfast? Let's eat and then you give me a tour of this big penthouse like you promised?"

Austin nodded and felt his gut twist when she visibly relaxed. Yeah, something was definitely up. Ordinarily, he wouldn't mince words but experience with Kylie showed she would only clam up — or worse, storm out — if he pressed the issue.

Instead, he took her hand and led her into the kitchen. A masterpiece of gleaming stainless steel and white marble, his kitchen was state-of-the-art.

"That was delicious," Kylie said around a mouthful of scrambled eggs topped with fresh cilantro, avocado, and sautéed onion. She took a sip of the orange juice then sighed, rubbing her stomach. The movement lifted her top, revealing creamy, smooth skin.

"Glad I could satisfy," he teased.

196

"Seriously, where did you learn to cook?"

Austin's fingers tightened on the spatula before he shrugged, then leaned down to finish loading the dishwasher. "My grandfather."

"Sounds like you were close."

Austin swallowed. "Very. He practically raised me." His throat closed and he felt tension creep into his shoulders. He almost jumped at the soft press of Kylie's head against his back. They stayed that way until he shifted.

"Come on. Let me give you that tour. If you're going to be coming around more often, you need to know where everything is."

He led Kylie throughout the penthouse, finally stopping outside a room with a fingerprint scan panel. Of the three floors they'd gone through, this was the last of the rooms. It was on the lower level, the same level as the indoor pool.

"That's where the millions are made," Kylie spoke softly, but there was an odd note in her voice that made him glance over. She looked nervous, but her features smoothed when she caught him looking. She flashed a weak smile that made his internal alarm start ringing.

Shaking off the feeling that she was holding something back, Austin squeezed her hand. "Some of them. This is my private server room." At her startled look, he continued,

"Most of the business files are kept on internal servers but files that really matter to me, like this new project, are kept here. It's basically hack-proof. Brixton thinks I'm paranoid, but you can never be too careful."

Kylie swallowed, her gaze unfocused as her hand went to the neck of her borrowed top. Trying to lighten the mood, he added, "Of course, if I took you inside, you'd know all my secrets and then I'd have to kill you. You understand, of course."

"Of course." Her voice sounded strange. Then her gaze focused on him and the emotion glittering there made him suck in a breath. Her fingers flicked open her top, revealing more temptingly bare skin. "Now I have to confess."

"What?" He couldn't look away from the movement of her fingers.

"Since you've given me this tour of your lovely home, I've only had one thing on my mind."

"Tell me." He swayed toward her.

"I have a fantasy. I'm afraid you'll judge me if I tell you."

"Tell me anyway," Austin rasped, backing her against the server room door. She bit his ear.

"I can't stop thinking about you taking me in each and every one of these rooms."

"There *are* a lot of rooms," he murmured, trailing his lips over her throat, leaving a trail of goosebumps on her skin.

Leaning back, he noticed the intensity of her expression. Something was wrong. Her desire for him had always been intense but the way she gripped his arms, the way she arched into him — it all held an edge of desperation. Did it have something to do with the phone call earlier?

I really am too paranoid. He trusted Kylie. More than he'd trusted any woman since Delilah. That was enough to move his fingers to the scanner, letting them into the server room.

"Welcome to my inner sanctum," he murmured into her hair. She shivered but stepped further into the room only to shriek when an electronic voice spoke.

"Hello, Mr. DeAngelis. The heat signature in the room indicates that, besides your biometrics, an unauthorized person has entered the room."

Austin had to laugh at Kylie's startled expression. "That's Niaexa, she is here for extra security. Let me take care of that." The last thing he wanted was for the A.I. to keep interrupting — or worse, to start narrating — when he was busy doing God knows what to Kylie.

He sat in a chair in front of a bank of terminals, half listening as Kylie wandered around the room. At her snort, he glanced back to find her eyeing the bed in the corner. When she raised her eyebrow, he shrugged.

"Sometimes I get caught up working here. It makes sense to be comfortable. Done," he declared, hitting a final key. He started to rise, only to groan when Kylie settled in his lap, the fullness of her bottom pressing against his crotch.

"Take me to bed, Austin. Make me yours."

The feel of her mouth against his pushed aside all doubts. Grasping her thighs, he carried her to the bed and did just that.

Kylie checked Austin's sleeping form and slowly slipped out of bed. Her naked toes touched the cold tile floor. Goosebumps rose on her skin. The temperature in the room was moderated by some electronic contraption to ensure that the computers and circuits were kept cool. She would have been cold anyway, so cold. Not bothering to dress, Kylie made her way towards the unlocked computer screen. Looking over her shoulder, she checked that Austin was still asleep. She plugged in the thumb drive, hit a few keys, and let the program do its work. In what felt like hours, she was both relieved and dismayed when a glance at the screen showed that the download was complete.

Ejecting the device, she clutched it in her clenched fist. Although the distance from the bed to the PC was short, it felt like the world had ended and begun again in the time it took for her to creep back quietly to her spot. Sweat trickled down between her naked breasts and her heart beat twice its normal speed. She felt panic taking over. What if Austin awakened? What if she was caught? More than the prospect of going to jail, it was the thought of Austin's disappointment that terrified her most. She never wanted him to look at her with disappointment, not now, in this moment when she realized she loved him. There it was — the truth. She loved Austin DeAngelis; loved him like she'd never loved anyone. She loved the fact that with his many blessing and gifts, he was still humble, still vulnerable, and still open.

Despite his power, the vulnerability she sensed in him spoke to the vulnerability in her. They were similar in the fact that they both went to great lengths to hide their fragility. They'd both suffered and had learned to live with the shell they placed around themselves for protection. That she now wanted to show Austin all of herself and wanted him to see the person she kept hidden from everyone, was the universe's way of playing a cruel joke on her. Just when she'd met a man she wanted to give...everything, it was a man she was determined to betray.

It was all Kylie could do to stop herself from weeping. But she was a realist. She'd lived with hard decisions before. She'd survived when life didn't go her way and would do so again. She had to. That her parent, the person who'd given her life, was the person responsible for all her unhappiness was her payment for what she must have done wrong in another life. She hated her father. She wanted to see him rot in jail for what he was doing. Instead, she would probably be the one in prison. She would be the one who had to live with the consequences while Soldier did what he did best...disappear.

Kylie gripped the thumb drive tighter, pulled away the sheet and lay down. She wanted to be far away when he awoke but that would cause suspicion. If she was lucky, when the theft was discovered, maybe they wouldn't know exactly who it was. The fact that the theft would destroy Austin's company was moot. She had one more night to sleep in his arms; one more night to feel his heat, warmth, and breath as it caressed her skin. She had another night of being where she wanted to be, safe and loved in Austin DeAngelis' arms. She hugged him tighter, pushed her breasts against his back, sighed, closed her eyes, and prayed for sleep.

Chapter Sixteen

There she was. Austin ran his fingers through his hair and resisted the urge to let frustration and fury tighten his fingers enough to wrench the silver strands. Despite the amazing evening followed by an even more incredible daybreak, the last couple of days Kylie had been scarce. He rewound the footage again and let the video play for what felt like the millionth time. Even though nothing on the screen had changed, he still doubted and couldn't accept the evidence of his eyes. Instead of concentrating on the things his mind didn't want to accept, like the way Kylie crept out of his bed and invaded his privacy so she could steal from him, he concentrated on the things he enjoyed seeing. Like the fact that Kylie had been naked as she did the deed. She'd left his arms, his bed, and his body heat in a mission to ruin him and his company but had done so completely naked. He admired her for that. She was a thief and completely untrustworthy, but she was a corrupt and beautiful thief. He'd forgotten to disable the camera along with the security system. It was his failsafe. She would have gotten away with the theft scot-free if it wasn't for this video evidence.

He should call the police, wanted to, should have already done so, but the man in him hesitated to turn over the evidence. How the cops would love to replay the evidence, rewind, replay, rewind, and replay. All of them would get hard just watching Kylie creep from the bed in nothing but her skin. More than that though, he could imagine Kylie's mortification at being put on public display. How a woman so private would feel knowing she was the object of lust, the deliberate armor her everyday clothes provided, violently stripped away; her nakedness immortalized on video. She wouldn't recover. She'd be damaged by it. Changed. He couldn't do it to her. He wanted to. She deserved it for what she'd done, but he'd find another way to make her pay.

Austin turned away from the footage, he couldn't watch anymore, but still couldn't stop asking himself why she'd done it. Money, of course, but he thought he knew her. He didn't think something like money motivated Kylie.

He'd been wrong. He'd been wrong about a woman before. It was *that* knowledge that burned a trail of fire down his chest, causing it to ache. Would he never learn his lesson? When would it sink in that no woman had ever loved him for himself? There was always a motive involved. He served a purpose and was a means to an end. It served him right. He'd let his guard down around Kylie. Her deception was a brutal way of being reminded of that, but he deserved it for being a gullible fool. He wouldn't be that foolish again. He picked up the phone.

"Mr. DeAngelis, it's highly unusual for a department to set up a high-end sting operation without the proper evidence. If you'd just let us see the video," Detective Francis of the Ontario Provincial Police said, frustration lacing his words.

Austin knew he was being unreasonable but the reasons he didn't want to turn over his surveillance video hadn't changed. Kylie had to be caught and punished but he couldn't bear to do it by revealing the video. There had to be another way. He'd catch her in the act; if for no other reason than to be able to look her in the eyes when she realized that he was on to her; that the freedom she prized would disappear when she was behind bars. He wanted to see the betrayal first-hand. He also wanted to know her accomplices. Did she have a lover? Who else would benefit from this deception? She couldn't have set up this high-level scheme on her own. She'd had to have help. He wanted to destroy everything that Kylie treasured and lay those broken pieces at her feet.

The rage running through his body scared him. She wasn't the first person who'd attempted corporate espionage. Many before her had been caught and left to rot in jail. Kylie, however, was the person who'd come the closest to succeeding. The first person who'd claimed to care for him as she stole from him. The first person he'd let his guard down around and felt he could trust. That was her crime. She could have stolen his program and made millions. He would have forgiven her more easily for that than what she'd actually accomplished stealing — his heart.

"Put a tail on her. I want to know who she's talking to. I want to know who she's meeting and when. If your department doesn't have enough resources for that, I have more than enough of my own. I can do it myself. I want the persons involved in this scheme caught. Is that understood?"

"Yes, Mr. DeAngelis. We'll catch all involved," the detective promised.

After talking with the police, Austin was heartsick. He needed answers. He needed to know what it was about him that made him so unlovable. So where did one go when they had nothing and no one? Where did one go when there were millions in the bank but not one genuine person on the earth who cared if he lived or died? One went to the source. He sat in the dark in the house. He didn't even blink when his mother walked into her living room and flicked on the lights.

"You're the reason why I pick women who don't want me. I'm my father's son," he said to her back.

"Austin!" Her hands flew to her heart as she spun towards him. "You scared me. What are you doing here?"

"Kylie's left me," Austin announced.

"That's good, isn't it?" his mother said, insensitive as always.

"Yes, good," Austin answered listlessly. "They all leave. First you, then Delilah, and now Kylie. The only ones that stay are the ones that want something. The ones I care about never stay."

His mother twisted her hands and seemed to fight with herself. "You liked...ah...loved this one then?" she asked, clearly uncomfortable with the personal direction the conversation had taken.

Austin didn't answer. He just looked up at her, his eyes clearly revealing the anguish he felt. He lowered his gaze and asked the question he'd asked her before. He'd never gotten

STEFANIE GRAHAM

an acceptable answer. "Why do you hate me? Why do they all hate me?" he asked, bewildered.

"I don't hate you, Austin!" His mother swung around and walked to the window. She kept her back to him. Wringing her hands, she spoke haltingly. "Don't you understand?" she asked, her shoulders slumping as if weighed down by a heavy weight. "How else could I make an affectionate and loving boy learn to stay away from me?" She turned to look at him. "You had so much love in you and you wanted to share that love with everybody, even me. That much was obvious about you from when you were young. No amount of rejection would keep you away from me. No amount of coldness would stop you from trying to engage me every time you saw me. Your father was starting to notice. He was starting to get jealous. Any type of jealousy on his part would have ended badly for you."

"I'm his son," Austin said, confused.

"No, you're his rival," his mother corrected him forcefully. "You were a boy growing into a man who would have demanded my time and affection. That would have made an enemy out of your father. I accepted early on who I married. I've resigned myself to paying the price for what my desire for riches has brought me. That doesn't mean you should have been forced to pay too. I happily abandoned you to Diavolo. He was the only person your father couldn't bully. Inside that old man was enough love for a whole arsenal of boys."

"He couldn't substitute for a mother's love, even though he tried," he told her, his shoulders slumping at the words.

"I know that, Austin, but I can't say that I am sorry," she said without remorse. "If I had to choose again, the outcome would have been the same. I have never been a very emotionally accessible woman. I don't give or receive love easily. It's partly why your father is so drawn to me. Finding ways past what he considers my armor is almost an erotic challenge for him. I've never loved him, but I love the lifestyle he has given me. Any finer feelings I claim to have, they belong to you. I loved you the best way I could. I hope you can accept that and move on."

The statement was delivered matter-of-factly, without inflection or apology, but Austin sensed that the words were his mother's way of pleading. The little speech was the most feeling communication he had ever received from her. The explanation didn't erase the bitterness he felt, or erase the neglect he suffered throughout his childhood, but knowing, finally, that his mother didn't think he wasn't worth loving helped. It helped to know that if she could love him in her own dysfunctional way, maybe other women could love him as well.

Austin got up and reached out towards his mother as he'd done many times before in anger; this time the embrace he offered, if not quite affectionate, was something else.

"Don't hug me!" Brinkley said almost frantically. She swallowed hard, her voice shaking. "Most of my life touch has been associated with discomfort. I want you to touch me. Need you to touch me, but I was afraid of tainting you with my defect as a boy, so I banned touch from our interactions. It was easier for me. It was not so easy for you."

Austin reached for her again.

"No!" she said wildly. Fear and panic were in her eyes. "Don't touch me." When she saw his expression, one she must have recognized from his youth, she tried again. Taking a deep breath, she reached out for him. Austin's hands remained at his sides. "Don't touch me," she repeated in a soft voice. "But if it's okay, I'd like to touch *you*." And with that, she reached out tentatively and ran her hands down his face, gingerly curled her arms around his waist, and slowly laid her head against his chest.

"Austin," she breathed his name into his chest to the tempo of his wildly beating heart.

"...Mother," Austin said in response. He was glad that the woman, who had never shown him any affection during his childhood, couldn't see the tears glistening in his eyes.

Kylie was done hiding. After days of laying low, not being able to face herself in the mirror, she made a decision. "Here, take it!" In the alley outside the company offices, Kylie shoved the thumb drive into her father's hands. He looked startled at first and then his shocked expression relaxed into a grin.

"You pulled it off already? That was quick." The smile widened. "I have to admit," he said, shaking his head, "I didn't think you'd be able to do it. I had my doubts you'd be able to con a man that rich and powerful, but I should have known. You're my daughter after all. Why look at you," he said. His perusal made her uncomfortable. "You have what it takes to rob men of their common sense. Good job, baby!"

"I'm not your baby, David. I wasn't when I was young enough for that name and I'm not now. That we share any type of DNA makes me sick. Take the thumb drive, quit this job, and get out of my life. I never want to see you again."

If she thought her speech would have some kind of sobering effect on him, if deep in her heart she believed the thought of losing her would convince him to change direction, her hopes were dashed when he stared at her and simply shrugged.

"Where should I send your take?" He was all business.

211

"Send it to hell for all I care. I don't want anything to do with it or you. Get out of my sight. You make me sick."

"Sorry you feel that way, Kylie," he said. His gaze ran over her face as if he was memorizing her features. "With your looks and that little body of yours, we could have done amazing things together. A word of advice from your old man before I hightail it out of here. Don't try to stay around long enough to beg that man for any kind of forgiveness. He won't give it. Once he's been burned, a man like that will never let you get near him again. Let it go and find someone your own speed. From the beginning, he was way out of your league."

With that, he threw the thumb drive in the air and caught it in his fist. He saluted her, turned on his heel and was gone. Had he bothered to spare her a glance, he would have seen the devastation his words left behind.

Kylie was a wreck. She'd just betrayed the man she loved, and for what? So Soldier could get rich? Her mother wouldn't have wanted that. She would never have agreed with her plan to do what Soldier wanted for the sake of her health. She would have convinced Kylie to find another way. She'd done what she had to do but didn't feel good about it. She'd turned her options over in her mind, but no solution left her with Austin. The lies she'd told were unforgivable. He'd had so much betrayal in his life already that how could he look at her with anything other than contempt despite her motives? He couldn't. So, in the end, she'd done what she had to, done what she thought was right, and had to live with it.

"The drop was made, sir."

"She gave him the drive?" Austin asked.

"Yes, she did," the detective answered.

Inside Austin's chest, his heart ached. Somewhere he'd hoped that she wouldn't do it. Deep inside a small little part of him prayed that she cared for him, that there was an explanation for her treachery. Such hopes were for boys. Like a man, he had to take the truth the hard way.

"Awaiting your orders," the detective prompted.

"Wait until he delivers the drive to my competitors and then pick them all up. I don't want there to be any mistakes."

"Yes, sir." He nodded and left to join the team of detectives camped out in Austin's living room.

Austin looked out at them, pictured Kylie in cuffs, and lowered his head into his hands.

Chapter Seventeen

"Austin, I could have done this with Beatrice, but I hear she's out and won't be back for a while. I know it's unusual for me to go straight to the company owner, but I need to get this over with. I didn't see another way." Kylie took a deep breath. "I'd like to resign. I quit. I'm sorry to give such short notice but a great opportunity has come up and I can't let it go. I hope you understand."

Kylie let out a long shaky breath. Was her speech as long and loquacious as she thought? Was that her voice laced with as much anxiety and dread as she feared? Was that her in Austin's office at Avion just hours after her meeting with her father? Could he tell she was still having trouble meeting his gaze? She couldn't sit around and wait for the ax to fall, wait for Austin to discover her betrayal. She was a coward. All she could think to do was run. She'd grab her mother and take off. Surely, they could find some island where they could live quietly, and cheaply, for the rest of their lives.

She watched Austin stare at the piece of paper on his desk. He picked it up without a word and tore the document in half. "What did you think, Kylie? Did you think you could just come in here, hand me some document, and then disappear? This is *me*. Austin. You really thought you could walk out of my life just like that?"

Kylie hardened her heart. With effort, she raised her head and looked at her boss, the man she loved. With a voice gone cold, she said what he needed to hear.

"Boss, it's been a great ride, but I never promised you forever. If your feelings got tangled in this thing we had going, then I'm sorry. I never promised wedding bells. You're getting too attached, too needy, and I can't handle that. I'm leaving. Try to understand. One dick, every damn day, day-after-day was never my thing. You, of all people, should understand that variety is the spice of life. I'm off to explore more varied seasonings."

Austin didn't say a word. Instead, from where he sat, he pinned her with his gaze and started clapping. The sound of his hands coming together was loud in the room.

"A plus performance Ms. Derringer but I'm not buying it. Tell me what's wrong."

"Nothing is wrong!" she yelled, her nerves fraying under the pressure.

"...*Nothing*?" he repeated, calmly ignoring her outburst.

"My God, Austin," she exclaimed. "I said nothing." She rubbed her wet palms on her pants.

"Go then, Kylie." His face was devoid of expression as he dismissed her. "Good luck."

She froze at his easy acquiescence and then nearly ran from the room.

Kylie was gone but she wouldn't get far. It was after hours. Everyone was gone for the day — perfect timing. From what he could see from the open doorway leading to one of his small conference rooms, Beatrice, his HR Manager, sat surrounded by police and two members of his security team. Her hair was drooping around her shoulders and her mascara was running as tears ran down her face. Some women cried beautifully, Beatrice unfortunately, wasn't one of them. Bright red spots were prominent underneath the pale pallor of her skin. Her light powdery makeup was disturbed by the dark trails of mascara that ran from her eyes to her chin.

She was the leak in his security Austin thought as he looked at her from across the room. As the HR manager, she had access to sensitive data. From what he knew of her from their interactions, she was a serious, focused, and a career-conscious employee. He wondered what enticement had led her astray. He wondered what the culprit had offered her to make her betray both her boss and her morals. He didn't have long to wait to have his questions answered.

As he approached, Beatrice caught sight of him and leaped to her feet.

"Mr. DeAngelis!" she exclaimed, grabbing a hold of his hand and squeezing it tight. "He made me do it. He seduced me. He said he'd tell my husband Bobby John about our affair if I didn't cooperate. I couldn't let him ruin my marriage. I just couldn't!" she said earnestly, more tears gathering in her eyes. "I didn't mean for things to get this far but he kept on asking me do to more and more and I couldn't refuse. Please understand. I'm so sorry!" she said and began sobbing even harder.

Austin almost felt sorry for her — almost. Because of her, a project he'd invested in had almost landed in the hands of his competitor. She should have come to him. She'd chosen not to. He said as much, which set her off into another fit of crying.

"He's a devil, Mr. DeAngelis. He'll say anything and do anything to get what he wants. He's not above using any dirty trick to get his way. I thought getting him this job and rushing his clearance would be the end of it, but he kept on asking for more."

"Who is *he*, Beatrice?" Austin asked but he already knew the answer.

"Adrian Vanderline," she confessed bitterly. "I don't even know if that's his real name."

She didn't know his real name, but Austin did. At that moment, he realized why the man on his security team had always seemed so familiar and understood why he'd questioned his presence on his team from the first moment he laid eyes on him. It was because he was familiar. It was because he reminded him of someone. It was because the beard couldn't disguise that he had the face of the woman Austin had thought he loved. He had Kylie's face and her eyes. Austin didn't know exactly their familial connection, but he guessed the man was the father she never spoke about.

For a fleeting moment, he wanted to convince himself that she'd been coerced into stealing from him, but just like Beatrice, she had no excuse. He'd spent weeks between her thighs. He'd learned every part of her anatomy, so he knew her pleasure points as well as he knew his own. They spent countless hours lounging in bed. She had too many opportunities to tell him that he had an enemy at his gate. His only conclusion at this stage in the game was that she was in on it. The time she'd spent with him wasn't for pleasure; she was gathering information. She was using him so that she could get access to his secrets. Damn if she hadn't succeeded.

He'd been vulnerable with her like he'd never been with anyone else. He'd opened up to her. She'd succeeded in penetrating his armor as no one had since his college days. For being effectively sinister, diabolical, and outrageously sexy while doing it, she, and her whole family would have to pay and pay big. He wanted revenge. It wouldn't help heal the pain and humiliation he felt, but it would be a start.

From the entryway of his house, Austin saw the woman. She was carelessly draped sideways across his lounge chair. Her long, lean legs were encased in soul-stomping high heels, swinging back and forth in indolence. The woman's head was thrown back, her eyes closed, her hair loose and hanging down the side of the chair, almost sweeping the ground. She had on one of his button-up shirts, and from what he could tell, little else. In her hands, hanging from one curled fingertip, was a pair of steel handcuffs. His heart shouldn't have sped up and started beating erratically at the sight of her, but it did. He walked further into his house and didn't stop moving until he stood in front of the chair looking down at her.

"How did you get in?"

Kylie didn't open her eyes. "You told the concierge I could come swimming anytime. He let me in," she said in answer.

"I'll have to rectify that," Austin stated. "What are the handcuffs for?"

She opened her eyes then and looked at him. What he saw made him catch his breath. Kylie had never looked at him that way before. Her gaze was open, vulnerable, searching, sorrowful, and distraught. He read so many emotions in her eyes that he lost count. She held the handcuffs up.

"These are for you."

"I have ideas of what I could do with those cuffs, but I get the feeling you have something completely different in mind," he said peeling off his suit jacket and loosening his tie.

She stood up abruptly from the chair, walked over to him, and stood in front of him; her heels made her eyes level with his chin. She held her wrists together in front of him, palms up. "I'm turning myself in."

"What did you do?" Austin asked even though he already knew.

221

"I stole from you," she confessed. "I didn't want to do it, but no excuse would ever be good enough. I'm not going to beg. I just want you to know that I'm sorry."

"You don't seem sorry. You're dressed for seduction, not Sing-Sing," he observed dispassionately but his heart was beating.

"I cleaned up most of my mess, but I still might be gone for a long time. I was hoping you'd consider giving me something memorable for old times' sake."

The mess she'd made couldn't be cleaned, he thought. "What kind of memories would you like?" he said instead, casually eyeing her and observing how good she looked in anything that belonged to him.

"Make love to me," she said in a strained whisper. "Pretend that you love me and show me just this once what that would feel like."

Austin hesitated, and her face fell. She began to turn away and he grabbed the first thing he could get his hands on. It happened to be her hair. His hands tangled in the thick, wavy mass and he used it as a tether to gently but firmly pull her back to him. She plastered herself to him and he could feel the entire length of her. His tightening grip made her rise up on her toes. She flung her head back to ease the pressure. It brought her full, pouty lips almost close to eye level. He could see her pulse beating in her neck.

Austin bent low and caught the lobe of her ear between his teeth. He bit gently before soothing the spot with his tongue. She moaned and pressed more firmly against him.

"You've been a very bad girl." Fire and fury burned through him.

"I know," she said breathlessly. "Punish me."

"Oh, I want to. I really want to." He could hear the longing in his voice.

"Do it. I've been bad so very bad. I'm yours to do with what you want. Do anything. I won't complain."

"Offering cart blanche to a man like me is a very dangerous thing to do, Ms. DeValle."

"...Derringer," she said automatically like he knew she would. "My name is Derringer."

"No, it isn't, Kylie," he disagreed. "The minute you agreed to be the puppet for a man like...What's his real name?"

She didn't ask who. "...Soldier," she answered. "David," she corrected herself, her eyes filling with tears of regret.

"Yes, him. The minute you agreed to do his bidding, you became his spawn not in theory but in truth. You are his creation and you and he are exactly alike."

Kylie stumbled backwards on her high heels as his words struck her. Tears gathered in her eyes. "I am not my father's daughter, Austin. I am many things but not that. I am Kylie

Derringer. That man is nothing to me. That we even share blood is enough to make me sick."

...*Then why?* Austin screamed the words but only in his head. He would never say them aloud. He'd rather die first. If it was blackmail, force, or coercion, she could have come to him and they could have worked it out together. She chose not to do that. She was no longer his problem. Let the justice system decide what to do with her. He was finished. ...*Done.* He looked down at an erection that threatened to leap out from his pants. His mouth twisted wryly. It was a beautiful internal speech, but he was such a fucking liar. He wanted Kylie despite what she'd done. He wanted her. He desired her even now. He parted her shirt.

Her nipples were dark and dusky, a spellbinding contrast to her pale gold skin. They were like succulent raspberries, ripe for the picking. They reminded him in that moment of why he'd always loved fruit. Fruit like Kylie Derringer — sweet, tasty, and *tart* — was a delight to the tongue. He wanted to lick her, *devour* her. He wanted the taste of her on his tongue constantly. Being inside her made him happiest.

No deal he had ever closed, no prize he had ever won, no possession he had ever acquired, felt as good to him as when Kylie *came* and then fell asleep in his arms. He liked to look at her after he'd worked her over, after he'd wrung her dry, after she had screamed his name so loud and long that her voice was hoarse. He liked testing his stamina on her. How long could he go? How much of his big dick could she take?

He wanted her to obsess over him, to be the first thing she thought of when she woke up in the morning and the last before going to sleep at night. He wanted her consumed by him. *He*, on the other hand, wanted to retain control over his emotions. Kylie wasn't the kind of girl you fell in love with. She didn't want to be *possessed*. She would never do as she was told. She was scornful of relationships and distrustful of men and their motives. Falling for a girl that protective of her heart would be disastrous. Plus, he didn't do love. He saw what love did to people. He saw what being too obsessed with someone did to people and couldn't afford to be that guy.

It would have to be enough that Kylie craved him. It would have to be enough that he planned to enslave her and in doing so, have her with him always without having to risk his heart. For the first time in his life, he understood his father and that scared him. He understood wanting a woman so badly that it hurt. He knew now how that obsession could grow and get out of hand. He understood everything now. Now that it was too late, now that the plan had backfired. Now, when he was the one enslaved.

"Kylie, considering your crime, you took a chance coming here." He removed his hands from her body and shoved them in his pockets to keep from touching her. "With the millions of dollars you could have cost me, it would be within my rights to lock you in this room like a prisoner. I could do anything I wanted to you and get away with it. I could deny you food and water. Instead, I could just feed you dick as your only meal." His eyes gleamed with the thought.

"Sounds like a prison made in heaven to me," Kylie said, her gaze hot.

He removed his clenched fists from his pockets, held her shoulders, and pushed her towards the door. "Get out."

"What?" She looked startled, her eyes still glassy with desire.

"Get out," he repeated, so they would both know he meant it. "Don't go far. The police will be around shortly," he snapped. "What did you think, Kylie? Did you think you could fuck your way into a lighter sentence?" Austin grabbed her jacket that was flung across his couch and threw it at her. She took it and left quietly.

Chapter Eighteen

Austin entered the lobby of his office building early the next morning and headed towards the elevators. He wore an expertly tailored, three-piece, navy-and-white Brioni pinstripe suit. His Berluti leather shoes gleamed, his hair was styled to perfection without a strand out of place and he'd dusted off his Maybach and drove himself to work. He should have felt good. In control. He felt like shit. The bags under his eyes, the tight line of his lips, and the slightly grey pallor of his skin from too much bourbon told its own tale. He hadn't slept last night after he'd thrown Kylie out and was in a terrible mood. His mood darkened further when he was met halfway to his destination by the detective he'd been working with. He was with two uniformed police officers.

"Good morning, Mr. DeAngelis. Can we have a word?" The words were polite but there were signs of strain in the man's eyes.

"Of course, Detective Francis," Austin agreed. Before he'd had his coffee, talking was the last thing he wanted to do. "What can I do for you? I'm assuming you have news," he said.

"Yes, we have news. Not good news I'm afraid." The detective shifted uncomfortably.

Austin raised an eyebrow but didn't speak.

"We've lost him, sir." Detective Francis shoved his hands into his pockets.

"You did what?" Austin's voice dripped steel.

The detective gulped and adjusted his collar nervously. "We had our best guys on David DeValle, but he managed to allude us. Something must have tipped him off. Don't worry, Mr. DeAngelis, we'll get him."

"Did you at least recover the drive?" Austin asked, his tone clipped.

The officer shook his head. "I'm afraid not."

"What about the girl?"

The officer rushed to explain. "Without the drive or the suspect, we couldn't hold her. We picked her up, questioned her, but then she was released."

Austin swore viciously. He moved to turn away when a commotion at his front entrance halted him in place.

"Freeze!" an officer shouted.

"Freeze," another officer yelled, gun raised.

"Hands up. ...Freeze!" Detective Francis' voice and raised gun joined the others.

There were guns trained on a black man in aviator glasses and biker shorts. He had a gun in his hand and a... *hostage.*

"Kinky?" Austin couldn't believe his eyes. He began to walk forward but one of the officers tried to hold him back. Discounting his own safety, Austin shook him off and walked closer.

"Kinky, are you trying to get yourself killed?" Austin snapped. "Who the hell is that and why have you brought him here?" Focused on Kinky, he didn't recognize the man at his side. "Let him go and let's go to my office so we can talk about this."

Kinky's response was to press the revolver deeper into the man's side. The man yelled, "Can someone shoot this son of a bitch, please?"

Austin glanced at the man and noted his black hair, mustache, glasses, and his non-descript clothes. He didn't look like someone that could piss Kinky off enough to get himself shot.

Austin tried again as he saw the officers and the security team beginning to circle. "Let the guy go before you become a hashtag for Black Lives Matter," warned Austin. After the incident with Kinky and the police, he already had visions of him on a slab with a toe tag.

Kinky jabbed the gun further into the man's side. He jumped again. "...Shot? Why shoot me? He's the culprit. It's not my gun; it's his. He got all mean and violent when I told him I saw him talking to your girl once, so I knew he was up to something sneaky. When he realized I knew who he was, that's when he tried to use the gun on me, but I got the drop on him," he explained, his tone half boastful and half aggrieved. "Here I am saving the day and Toronto's finest wants to put me in a body bag. Ain't that some shit?" he said, his voice high with righteous anger.

"Kinky, you're not making any sense," Austin said. He edged closer, avoiding the officers who were trying to keep him back.

"No good deed goes unpunished." Kinky sighed again in frustration, and with that, he dragged the black hairpiece off the man's head and ripped the fake mustache from his now clean-shaven lip.

"Well, I'll be damned," the detective said before Austin could get the words out. "Lower your weapons," he commanded. The other officers reluctantly did what they were told.

"How the hell did you find him?" Austin asked in amazement.

Kinky smirked. "There are a million homeless people on the street and all those folks have eyes and ears. No one notices them, but they notice you. I had them keeping an eye on this fool after I figured out he was the one that called the cops on me. I wasn't about to forgive that shit easily. He was about to skip town. I patted him down with my fists before we got here." Kinky held up the drive. "Someone please tell me there's some kind of reward for this?"

"You can't hold me on that," DeValle protested. He struggled against the cuffs the officers had placed on his wrist. "That treacherous girl gave me bogus files. She's to blame for all of this. You can't pin anything on me and make it stick!"

"What?" Austin said, grabbing him by the shirt. The older man's eyes, no longer a dull brown but the same gray as his daughter's, flared wide.

"I'm innocent," he repeated. "There are no useful files on there. Never were. The bitch double-crossed me."

The words were barely out of DeValle's mouth before Austin slammed his fist into his jaw. He hit the floor, out cold.

Kinky whistled in admiration. "Still got that nice right hook from high school I see. Damn *son*, I'm feeling kind of proud of you right now."

"Where is she?" Austin demanded. There was desperation in his tone. He had to find Kylie. He had to make things right.

Kinky threw his hands up. "Damn if I know. You expect a body to do every damn thing around here?" Kinky was still muttering to himself when Austin ran to Detective Francis and grabbed him by his collar, nearly lifting him off his feet.

"Where is she?" Austin demanded again his hands shaking where he gripped the detective's lapel.

Francis peeled Austin's grip off his shirt and looked him in the eye. "If you mean that one's kid," he gestured to DeValle still lying prone on the floor. "She slipped her detail. Her mother is recovering in a nearby hospital. My guess is that she won't go anywhere without seeing her first."

Austin didn't ask any more questions; he was already running through the door.

Kylie hadn't understood the extent of her feelings for Austin until now. Now she knew for certain that the emptiness inside her, the yawning, deep, cavernous hole she thought she'd never be able to fill had an antidote. With the man she loved, the all-consuming loneliness born out of self-imposed seclusion; and a feeling of always being separate didn't have to be a lifetime condition. For a moment she'd known what it felt like to have someone come to her rescue, someone to lean on with the expectation that they could bear the weight of her fears and insecurities. Austin was a man up to the challenge and that thought had scared her. She knew if she let herself love him even a little bit, like all the things in her life, it would come crashing down all around her. Like it had. She couldn't bear for him to be a disappointment. She'd been disappointed enough. It hadn't mattered in the end though. She'd fallen in love with him and they'd disappointed each other.

"Go to him, Kylie. Explain," her mother urged her from her hospital bed.

"I can't. I won't," Kylie said, tucking sheets around her mother's body. She looked frail. She'd lost weight and finding out about Soldier's treachery had aged her. Kylie had been forced to confess just in case the police came looking for her. She wasn't naive enough to think a blank drive meant she was free. A thief was still a thief.

Kylie looked down at her pastel pink dress and clear heels. She dragged a hand through her flowing hair before twisting it back up in a knot. Looking like a suburban housewife had bought her the time she needed to slip her obvious surveillance detail. She didn't need accusing eyes or scrutiny while she spent time with her mother.

"Let's not talk about this. Let's talk about the fact that you, *young lady*, came out of surgery with flying colors." She was determined to focus on the positive. "Austin still may prosecute me for what I've done, but if I sell my studio that should pay for a decent lawyer and some of your needs until I figure something out."

"Oh, Kylie. I wish you had spoken to me before you stole from him in the first place," her mother said aggrieved. "I could just kill that bastard. Your father I mean, not Austin. I think Austin is quite lovely."

Kylie chuckled. She kissed her mother's cheek, suppressing tears of relief when she saw that the pain medication was already working. Her mother was asleep. She quietly left the room. Austin DeAngelis was standing outside. She didn't ask how he found out where she was.

"Do you have your cuffs with you?" Kylie asked in all seriousness.

"They're at home. I'm saving them for a special occasion." His gaze skimmed her outfit and he smiled at her, but it didn't reach his eyes. "I'll let you use them when we enter your dominatrix phase." He stepped forward, reaching for her hands. "Kylie, forgive me," he pleaded, his expression open.

Kylie looked at him and caught her breath. It was as if she was looking at him for the first time. She looked at him, not like he was her employer, or as she viewed most men, like a nuisance whose attentions she had to tolerate. She looked at him, not as a reminder of what Soldier was, but with the eye of a woman who, unlike her, came from a family who knew how to love without making it hurt. What she saw in his expression made her heart flutter wildly, but she couldn't trust herself or him, they'd hurt each other too much.

"Forgiven," she said, turning away. "Goodbye, Austin."

He grabbed her hand and placed it against his heart. "Not goodbye, Kylie. Never goodbye."

"What do you want from me?" she asked her composure slipping. She loved him so much.

"The drive was blank. Why?" he asked instead.

Kylie shrugged. "The drive's not blank. It has plenty of stolen files on there. I have it at home. I decided at the last moment not to give Soldier what I'd taken until I could figure something out. Make no mistake; I was just buying some time with the fake. I had every intention of betraying you, but I couldn't do it in the end. You deserved better. So did I. So, you see Mr. DeAngelis, no forgiveness required."

Austin gripped her hands in his. "I think you're wrong there, Kylie. I think you should forgive yourself for not being sure enough of my feelings for you to come to me for help. As always, you had to tackle this problem on your own. That's about to end. I think you should forgive me for not telling you how I feel."

"I know how you feel. You want me." Her tone implied she wasn't happy about it.

"I don't want you," he contradicted his face serious and intent. "Want is subjective. I don't want you, Kylie. I need you. I don't know when you became so important to me, but I can't picture my life without you. Move in with me. If that's not enough, then I have no objection to you wearing my last name along with my shirts every morning."

"What!" Kylie exclaimed, shocked.

"Oh, you didn't hear me?" He pulled her closer and pressed his mouth against her ear so the words tickled her eardrum. "Let's go back to my place and make love and then figure out how to make a life together. Move in with me. Marry me. Today. Next week. Next year. Whatever suits you. All you need to know is that I've never loved anyone as much as I love you. I knew that early on, but I was afraid of your effect on me. I don't care if marriage isn't in the cards for you. I'm not going to stop asking until you agree. Marry me, Kylie."

"I can't," she protested, finally finding her voice.

"Is it the police? They'll have more questions, but I'll get you the best lawyer in the nation to work that out. The only answer I will accept from you about my proposal is, *yes, I will*," he commanded.

She pulled away and put some needed space between them. "No, I really can't," she insisted. "I'm not the kind of woman you want."

"I'll be the judge of that," Austin argued with conviction.

The beginnings of a smile curved Kylie's lips. "No, I mean it. I can't. You'll want a wife who will wear a white dress on her wedding day. My Goth sensibilities can't agree to that." The smile transformed itself into a full-blown grin.

Austin got down on one knee and held her hand in his. The nurses milling around stopped to stare. "Marry me, Kylie and I'll buy you a black diamond. We'll have Bon Jovi play *You Give Love a Bad Name* at our wedding. I'll have Betsey Johnson design you a dress that's punk, Goth, and chic. If that's not enough, I will get a tattoo somewhere on my body to show you that I'm yours. Agreed?"

Kylie lovingly ran her fingers through hair the color of moonbeams and nodded. "Agreed."

Author's Note

I hope you have enjoyed reading *Pistol Whipped* as much as I enjoyed writing it. If you have, please consider leaving a review at the major sites such as Amazon and Goodreads. It's the greatest gift you can give an author, and I would very much appreciate it. I love hearing from readers and your recommendations are a wonderful way for booklovers to discover great new novels.

Thank you,
Stefanie Graham